All they'd had was one incredible night together four months ago.

Of course, they had both just wanted a moment of fun. They'd agreed to just enjoy themselves, no deep conversations.

And they had.

Just thinking about it made his blood heat and his body thrum with desire, but then he had to remind himself that they weren't in Spain anymore. He was her boss; she was the nurse working for him.

Sharon sighed. "I'm not sick, Dr. Varela. I know what's wrong with me."

"What's wrong, then, because I am concerned," he said.

"I'm pregnant."

He could feel the blood drain from his face. "Pregnant?"

"Four months," she stated, blushing.

"Four…" He trailed off as it h

Sharon nodded. "Yes, contacted me usi could have tol found out toda

He took a step ba

He couldn't quite be

She was pregnant and the child was his.

Dear Reader,

Thank you for picking up a copy of Sharon and Agustin's story, *Nurse's Pregnancy Surprise*.

This book was a lot of fun to write, but during a difficult time. It was a great escape and I hope that you will think so too.

Sharon has been through a lot in her life. She's learned to rely on herself and she certainly doesn't believe in a happily-ever-after, but at a conference in gorgeous Spain, she decides to take a chance on one night. She just didn't think it would lead to forever.

Agustin is a widower. His life is his work. But after a one-night stand, he can't get the beautiful Sharon out of his mind. Imagine his surprise when she turns up at his practice in Ushuaia, Argentina, practically the edge of the world, and she's pregnant with his child!

I hope you enjoy Sharon and Agustin's story!

I love hearing from readers, so please drop by my website, www.amyruttan.com.

With warmest wishes,

Amy Ruttan

NURSE'S PREGNANCY
SURPRISE

AMY RUTTAN

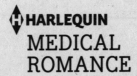

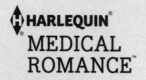

HARLEQUIN®
MEDICAL
ROMANCE™

Recycling programs
for this product may
not exist in your area.

ISBN-13: 978-1-335-73796-0

Nurse's Pregnancy Surprise

Copyright © 2023 by Amy Ruttan

For questions and comments about the quality of this book, please contact us at CustomerService@Harlequin.com.

Harlequin Enterprises ULC
22 Adelaide St. West, 41st Floor
Toronto, Ontario M5H 4E3, Canada
www.Harlequin.com

Printed in U.S.A.

Born and raised just outside Toronto, Ontario, **Amy Ruttan** fled the big city to settle down with the country boy of her dreams. After the birth of her second child, Amy was lucky enough to realize her lifelong dream of becoming a romance author. When she's not furiously typing away at her computer, she's mom to three wonderful children, who use her as a personal taxi and chef.

Books by Amy Ruttan

Harlequin Medical Romance

Portland Midwives

The Doctor She Should Resist

Caribbean Island Hospital

Reunited with Her Surgeon Boss
A Ring for His Pregnant Midwife

Reunited with Her Hot-Shot Surgeon
A Reunion, a Wedding, a Family
Twin Surprise for the Baby Doctor
Falling for the Billionaire Doc
Falling for His Runaway Nurse
Paramedic's One-Night Baby Bombshell
Winning the Neonatal Doc's Heart

Visit the Author Profile page
at Harlequin.com for more titles.

For my dear friend Desiree Holt. You once said I brightened your life, being your friend.
You brightened mine. As a new writer, you were one of the first big authors to befriend me.
You never competed; you only shared your knowledge. You were a light. I shall miss you.
Fly free, my dear sweet friend.

CHAPTER ONE

Barcelona, Spain

"SHARON, THAT HANDSOME stranger is staring at you again."

Sharon looked up from her book and glanced up to where her roommate at the medical conference she'd been attending was pointing. Her heart skipped a beat as she found him, sitting at the bar.

Everywhere she went this week she ran into him. He said his name was Gus, when they first met in the hotel elevator. She knew he was in the medical profession. This was a medical conference after all, and they were in several workshops together.

They always chatted, always compared notes after a workshop, and whenever she saw him she would feel a bubble of excitement inside her.

He was the most handsome man she'd ever seen.

Sharon had to remind herself that she was at this conference for work and not pleasure, but when she saw him, Gus the stranger with the sparkling dark eyes, her insides melted just a bit.

He made her feel things and think of things that were totally out of character for her.

Angelina grinned and elbowed her. "I know you're leaving tomorrow, but you should totally talk to him."

"I have talked to him before," Sharon replied, trying to tear her gaze away from his piercing blue eyes.

Angelina looked shocked. "What?"

"We've been in the same workshops. Infection control, postanesthesia care…another one about infections."

Angelina wrinkled her nose. "I remember those workshops. Kind of gross."

Sharon chuckled. "I thought you were a nurse?"

Angelina ignored her. "So, is he a doctor or a nurse?"

Sharon shrugged. "Not sure. The only thing I know is he's from Latin America. Somewhere."

"Did he tell you?" Angelina asked curiously.

"No, but we both figured out our Spanish accents are similar. Though his is more like my family's than mine is. Mine is tainted by New York." Sharon smiled at that. Although she hadn't divulged she was from Argentina to him, she'd been born there, but her Spanish was a mix of United States and Tierra del Fuego where her mother's family came from. Her father was Italian and she could speak that fairly well too.

When you traveled a lot, which she did for work, it was handy to know multiple languages.

Gus had been impressed when she mentioned that, but they didn't go too deep into personal stuff. That wasn't what she was here for.

What are you here for, then, besides work? He's the first guy you've noticed in years. Maybe you should have some fun.

She shook that thought away.

Heat crept up her neck and she really hoped that the blush didn't reach her cheeks. She had been planning to spend these last few days in Barcelona after this conference. She never really entertained the notion of a fling, but she had been feeling a bit lost lately.

She wanted some things in her life to change. She wanted to live a little.

A fling with a handsome stranger in Spain was definitely out of the ordinary.

As far as Sharon was concerned, Mr. Right was never coming, because she wasn't looking for him. She didn't believe in happily-ever-afters or love.

It's not like she had to do anything tonight.

It might be nice to flirt with him one last time.

And Gus wasn't a complete stranger. She knew his name. She knew he was smart, quiet and focused about medicine.

Things she appreciated and admired.

They didn't need to get into specifics.

"So you know him. Go talk to him!" Angelina urged.

"I don't know," Sharon said.

Angelina rolled her eyes. "Oh, come on. You told me you wanted a holiday fling once. Here's your chance. Don't be RPN Sharon Misasi tonight. Seduce him."

Sharon snorted. "Seduce him? What're you talking about? I can't."

"Sure you can. He clearly likes you, and what's there not to like about him?"

Angelina was right. Gus was very easy on the eyes.

He was tall, athletic, with a dark brown mop of curls and a strong bronzed jaw. Though that wasn't what did it for her the first time they met in that elevator. It was his eyes. His dark brown eyes not only sparkled, but when they settled on her it felt like she was the only one he could see. They mesmerized her, drew her in and made her blood heat with the promise of something more.

Every time she met his gaze he made her melt.

Just a little.

Every.

Single.

Time.

Yet there was something behind that facade of confidence, something sad that drew her to him. Like they shared something deep. She didn't know what, but she couldn't find out. No matter how good-looking or charming or appealing he was, she didn't have time for relationships or the opposite sex. Her career was too important, which had been the main complaint of the couple of men she'd dated for a short time.

Besides, she'd seen the negative effects of loving someone so much and how it could shatter your whole world when that person was gone. It was devastating. Even to the point of abandoning your own child because they reminded you too much of your deceased partner.

Sharon sucked back the memories of her childhood that were threatening to cloud her mind.

Romance was not for her.

So why was Gus so different? Why did he make her want to take a chance? She wasn't sure.

She wanted to find out though.

It would only be for one night. She'd be gone onto her next job and he'd move on as well.

Sharon stuffed her book into her purse and picked up her drink, with Angelina silently cheering her on. She trembled slightly as she made her way through the crowded hotel bar toward him.

He grinned when he saw her, those dark eyes sparkling. A dark curl on his bronzed forehead escaped between his fingers as he raked his hand through his thick hair.

"Gus?" she asked, hoping her voice didn't crack with nerves.

"*Hola*, Sharon," he replied, brightly.

"Yes." She liked the way he said her name. It rolled off his tongue. "Mind if I join you?"

"No. Not at all." He got up, pulling out the

bar stool next to him. She caught a whiff of his cologne. It was a crisp, clean scent. Subtle, but still manly.

Warmth crept up her neck and she cleared her throat as she sat down. She turned her back to him to try to regain composure.

"Thank you," she said, hoping her voice wasn't shaking.

Why did he make her so nervous? What was it about him?

"So how are you enjoying Barcelona?" he asked.

"It's great. But I haven't seen much of it with work."

He cocked an eyebrow. "What?"

She shrugged. "I've been busy."

He nodded. "I do understand that. Work is my life too."

"That sounds depressing, doesn't it?"

He grinned. "It does rather."

"So would you like to grab a drink?"

He turned and motioned to a waiter. "Yes, I like that."

"Maybe we could not talk..." Sharon trailed off as she noticed the waiter coming toward them. He was sweating profusely. It was a warm day, but not hot enough to be that sweaty.

Gus seemed to notice too, because his gaze narrowed and he sat up straighter.

"Are you okay?" Sharon asked the waiter gently.

"I'm fine," the waiter stated, but his balance was off and he was teetering to one side.

"I don't think you're fine, my friend," Gus said, standing up.

"Señor..." The waiter winced and then stumbled over, collapsing.

Gus helped him down on the ground. Sharon crouched down.

"Is he okay?" she asked.

"I think he's having a heart attack." Gus went over the man's vitals.

"You're a doctor?" Sharon asked, calmly.

"Sí." Gus frowned. "He's not breathing." He started compressions as she asked a nearby waiter to call an ambulance. Another staff member rushed over and gave her an AED device. She quickly began to work around Gus's compressions.

"What do you do?" Gus asked, glancing up.

"I'm a registered nurse practitioner. I've worked many a triage."

Gus nodded as he continued his CPR. "Excellent."

He stopped compressions as Sharon hooked

up the last of the electrodes to allow the AED to do its work. The device instructed her to shock the patient.

"Clear," she stated, making sure no one was touching the patient.

The AED shocked him, then instructed on its screen for Gus to continue compressions.

They continued in this way until the waiter's heart started and he was breathing again. The paramedics arrived and Gus and Sharon stepped back to let them do their work to transport the waiter to the hospital. The bar had been cleared out and shut down.

"It's good he had a heart attack in a bar with a doctor," Sharon remarked.

Gus nodded. "He was very fortunate. Not many are."

"No," she said, quietly.

"Should we go elsewhere for a drink?" he asked.

"Yes. Please." She could definitely use a drink after the excitement.

Gus opened his mouth to say something further when his phone buzzed. He frowned and cursed under his breath at the message.

"Sharon, forgive me, but I have to run."

Sharon was disappointed. "No problem."

"How about dinner in an hour? I know a great place and it's not far from here."

"Dinner?" she asked.

"If you're not busy."

"I'm not."

He grinned. "Great. Cafe Pacífica by the waterfront at eight o'clock."

"Okay," she said, nodding quickly.

He stepped closer to her. She pulled her cardigan tight around her and her heart began to race. He towered over her, which was strange as she was fairly tall herself at five foot nine.

"I'll see you then," he whispered huskily.

That dark promise laced in his voice made her weak in the knees—there was a part of her that was imagining all sorts of things in that simple answer.

It felt like he stood there for an eternity, before he stepped away from her and left the bar.

When he was gone, she took a deep breath to calm her nerves.

Gus made her nervous like no one had before. In a good way, but also in a way that scared her, because she was curious. She thought maybe she shouldn't show up to dinner.

Go out to dinner with him.

This was her chance at having a fling. A no-strings-attached night of passion. Something she could look back on fondly as a moment where she took a chance.

What harm could that do?

This was a big mistake. She wasn't going to come.

Agustin wasn't sure what had come over him.

Usually, he would casually date, but it never meant anything. He wasn't interested in finding a happily-ever-after. He'd had that before.

Once was enough.

The idea of loving another as much as he loved his late wife was unfathomable, because the thought, the mere idea of the pain he felt when she died and he was powerless to do anything was something he never wanted to feel again.

It was why he'd left Buenos Aires and opened a practice in Ushuaia.

He'd put his whole past life behind him and started fresh.

Women he had affairs with, they were pretty, but he had nothing in common with them. Sharon was gorgeous, but there was something different about her. He had noticed that at the first workshop they attended together. He had ascertained she was American, but also sounded like she came from somewhere in Argentina, but he wasn't one hundred percent sure.

He couldn't help but wonder if she was from Argentina.

Like him.

Only he didn't want to know. He tried to keep her at a distance, but it was hard. She was intelligent, smart, beautiful and sexy. She had long, soft, chestnut hair that was always pulled back and he pictured over and over again what it would be like to undo her hair and run it through his fingers.

He often thought of that when he saw her.

Actually, if truth be told, he often fantasized about that, and of kissing her luscious pink lips. It thrilled him when she would smile, her gray eyes focused on him and the hint of pink in her olive skin.

It had been a long time since he'd been so enticed, so enraptured by a woman. Not since his late wife, and that was ten years ago.

There was a passionate creature hiding under that prim and proper facade of Sharon's. She was a mystery and despite everything, all the protections he put up to protect himself, he was drawn to her, and she didn't seem to care one iota that he was flirting with her.

Which made him want to know her all the more.

You're here on business. Not to flirt.

It had been a year since his late father had died and he'd stepped in to take care of his half sister. That was when his world changed again, and he was struggling.

This conference was supposed to be a quick trip to Spain. A medical conference to help boost his private luxury plastic surgery clinic back home in Tierra del Fuego. He wanted to make his clinic the premier spot for people to fly in and get surgery.

He hadn't expected to run into an intoxicating woman at the same hotel—or to continue running into her.

He was glad she'd come over for a drink. It was bad timing when that poor waiter had a heart attack, but she had acted so quickly. They worked seamlessly in that moment. Two strangers. She'd kept her head and worked with him. That waiter had survived. Then he got a message from his half sister, who was hating the boarding school in Buenos Aires he'd sent her to and had banned her boyfriend Diego from visiting. Again.

Agustin was annoyed he couldn't get to know Sharon in that moment, which was why he'd suggested dinner and he hoped she'd actually come. He wanted to do more than talk shop with her.

Although there was a part of him that didn't want to get to know her either.

Still, he hoped she'd come.

He wasn't sure if she would. Every time he heard a click of heels on the cobblestone or saw a tall woman with her hair color, his heart would catch.

Agustin kept hopeful but really, did he expect Sharon to actually show up? They were strangers in a foreign country.

"Hi," she said, catching him off guard.

She stood beside the table in a pink dress, her long dark hair falling over one of her bare shoulders. She wore flats, which explained why she had snuck up on him.

She was absolutely stunning. It took his breath away for a moment.

Then he remembered his manners and stood. "You came."

"I told you I would," she responded sweetly, cocking her head to the side. "I don't usually go back on my word."

"I'm glad to hear it." He pulled out the empty chair so she could sit down.

She sat down and his knuckles brushed the bare skin of her back. It sent a shiver of electricity through him, just that brush of his flesh against hers.

"I'm sorry if I'm late."

"No. You're not and it's quite all right."

He would've waited all night. Only he didn't say that out loud. He was just glad that she was here. He took his seat across from her, just staring at her—it was hard not to in the moonlight.

"This is a beautiful little café," she said. "You've been to Barcelona before?"

"*Sí.* Not for a few years. This place is one of my favorites."

"I haven't explored the city much."

"How long have you been in Barcelona?" Agustin asked.

"Just the week. For the conference."

"Same as me. Just a short trip for the conference," he said.

"So we're both here for the conference." She smiled and dropped her head in her hand. "This is the most tedious conversation ever."

He chuckled softly. "It's utterly boring."

Sharon laughed. "I suppose so, but it's not. I like work."

"I believe we were talking about that before the waiter collapsed," he said.

"How is he?" she asked, gently.

He admired her empathy. "Alive. You were brilliant."

"Hardly. It's what I'm used to. Besides, you're the doctor."

"I get it, but let's not talk about our work anymore."

"Good idea," she agreed.

Work had been his life for far too long.

Except when his late wife had been alive. Then he had been able to find the balance, but when she died, he gave every moment he could to work, until he burned out.

His spine stiffened.

He didn't want to discuss his late wife or think about her.

Not tonight.

Not here.

The waiter came over and Agustin ordered them some wine and tapas.

"I hope you don't mind me ordering," he said.

"No. It's fine. You know what's good. I'll trust you."

"Do you travel a lot?" he asked.

"Only for…" She blushed. "Work, which we agreed not to talk about."

He smiled. "That's right."

Sharon was charming.

"I've often thought of taking some time off and visiting family I haven't seen in a while."

"Why don't you?" he asked.

A pink blush tinged her cheeks. "I don't

know. I guess I really never just gave much thought to it."

"Maybe you should. The soul needs time to rest."

Her lips quirked in a smile. "Oh, I didn't know you were so poetic."

"Are you teasing me?"

"Perhaps."

He grinned and leaned across the table. "I have layers of depth. If only you were staying long enough to get to know me."

"Are you trying to blackmail me into staying, Gus?"

His eyes sparkled. "And if I was?"

"You don't know me," she said, the blush on her cheeks deepening. "I could be a monster."

"Are you?"

She smiled, but didn't say anything. The waiter came and poured them wine, then discreetly left. Sharon took a sip out of the wineglass. He was mesmerized by the way her lips parted and he really wished for that fraction of a second that he was that glass of wine and that her lips were on him.

"I seriously doubt that you're a monster," he said, breaking the spell that she was weaving over him.

"You doubt that?"

"I do. I would like to get to know you. Perhaps see more of you. You're one of the most beautiful women I have seen in a long time."

"You're leaving soon too," she said.

"True," he remarked. "Still…it is the truth."

"Beauty is skin-deep," she said quietly.

"I know, but there's something more I see in you."

"Well, that may be…but unfortunately more is something I can't give."

Agustin understood that too, but he did want to get to know Sharon better and that did terrify him slightly. He didn't want to open his heart to anyone else. Not after losing Luisa, his wife, and their unborn child—not after having his life shattered.

He didn't trust the fates not to be cruel again.

Sharon was dangerous to every careful wall he put up to protect himself from ever being hurt again. Still, there was just something about her. Something he couldn't keep away from. Perhaps he was a sucker for punishment.

Maybe he was just lonely?

He dismissed that thought.

"I understand," he said, quickly. "I am not looking for a relationship either. Just…you were someone I wanted to get to know. I am attracted to you, Sharon. I can't deny that."

She seemed relieved. "I am attracted to you as well, Gus. It's just…"

"Just what?" he asked.

A blush returned to her cheeks. "I'm not used to this. I'm not very good at this."

He grinned. "Well, I am."

She looked down, her hair sliding over her face in a sweet, endearing way. He longed to brush her hair away, touch her chin and drag her gaze back to him. He was surprised at how much he wanted to touch her all the time.

"Are you?" she whispered.

"Yes, so let's enjoy this night together. No promises. No deep conversations. Let's enjoy the city so when you leave Spain you'll have more than just memories of work to remind you of this beautiful place."

Sharon smiled, her eyes lighting up. "I like that. Yes. Let's do that."

They held up their wineglasses and cheered to their decision. A night of fun. He wanted to show her everything that Barcelona had to offer. For one night, he wasn't going to think about how to protect his heart or how much he desired her.

Tonight was going to be about fun, and if a little romance happened along the way, then he wouldn't be opposed to that.

He just couldn't promise her forever, but it

seemed like Sharon didn't want that either, which was a relief.

Agustin secretly wanted a chance at forever again. There was a hole in his heart that longed for family, for love and forever, but he just couldn't open his heart to that again.

He wouldn't lose at love again.

So tonight would have to be enough.

CHAPTER TWO

SHARON COULDN'T REMEMBER when she'd had so much fun.

Actually, she really didn't have much fun. There was her work and then home. She had a few friends, but it was hard to trust people, to open up to people. Her work, her career as a registered nurse working all over the world was what she could count on.

So going out with Gus, a stranger she had met at the conference, was highly unusual for her. It was also kind of liberating and fun. She enjoyed the workshops with him, but this was so much better.

Sharon was the kind of person who liked to plan things out, so it was a bit different for her to let go and go with the flow.

She certainly didn't go off with people she hardly knew, but with Gus she felt safe.

It was a bit unnerving.

Just relax.

And that was what she had to keep telling herself.

She just needed to breathe and relax.

This was her one chance to live.

She never planned to get married, and she didn't plan on settling down. She liked her life traipsing across the world as a nurse.

No one let her down and she didn't let anyone else down either. Even if she was a bit lonely.

So even though this wasn't her usual modus operandi, she was glad to be here just the same. It was a memory that she knew she was going to keep forever.

So that she could say, later on, that she'd lived.

After their tapas and wine at the Cafe Pacífica, Gus took her on a whirlwind tour of Barcelona at night.

Just like New York City, where she grew up, Barcelona had a nightlife.

The city was lit up and there was music and laughter.

It breathed with life.

How long have I been asleep?

"Where would you like to go?" Gus asked as they walked the bustling streets.

She was getting slightly overwhelmed with the crowds. "I don't know. Somewhere quiet?"

As if sensing that she was a little anxious about being in a big group of people, he slipped his arm around her wait. She could feel the heat of his body through the thin cotton of her dress and she hoped she wasn't trembling under his touch.

She liked his hand there, in the small of her back, protecting her.

You don't need protection.

Sharon ignored that thought.

"How about the beach?" he asked. "We can take a moonlit stroll down by the water."

"The beach? Which one?"

"Platja del Bogatell is nice." He stepped toward the street and hailed a cab.

A taxi pulled off and Gus rattled off instructions to the driver and then opened the door. She slid inside and then he climbed in beside her. His body pressed against hers in the back of the tiny cab.

"It won't be crowded there, will it?" she asked, as the cab driver raced through the streets of Barcelona.

"Not at this time of night. No sun for the sun seekers, but there will be people. You don't like crowds?"

"I should, shouldn't I. I'm from New York."

He cocked an eyebrow. "Really? I wouldn't have taken you for a New Yorker."

"And why is that?" she asked, curious.

"Your accent. It's American but also… something else."

"My mother was from South America. We moved to New York when I was very young. So yes, I guess you're right. I'm not really a New Yorker."

He smiled at her lazily, making her heart skip a beat. "See, not a New Yorker. Not at heart."

She laughed. "Well, I don't have a lot of happy memories there."

"Then we won't talk about that. Tonight is not a night for unhappy memories."

She smiled appreciatively. "What's it a night for then?"

"Fun." He grinned and he slipped his arm around the back of the seat, close to her shoulders. It was comforting to have it there. "Maybe we can catch the last of the sunset."

"That would be nice."

He smiled.

The cab driver wound his way through the Gothic Quarter, past the Parc de la Ciutadella, and let them off near the stone walkway that ran along the length of the beach.

Sharon helped pay for the cab driver, who thanked them with a simple "*gracias*" before driving away to find another fare.

Gus was right, the beach wasn't completely deserted. There were a few dusk volleyball games happening and several people walking along the shoreline.

They wandered down to the water's edge. Gus kicked off his shoes and she set hers down next to his on the sand.

They were just in time to see the sun sink over the western horizon of the Mediterranean Sea. It was red and emitted an orange hue over the turquoise waters and the white sand beaches. It had been some time since she really stopped and watched a sunset or even a sunrise.

She couldn't remember the last time she did.

"Beautiful," she whispered.

"It is."

She glanced up to see that Gus was not looking at the sunset, but her. Warmth spread through her body again. She was overwhelmed and shy at the moment, which was also unlike her. The water lapped at her toes.

Her heart was racing and she wasn't sure about what she was thinking.

All she knew, in that moment, was she wanted him to kiss her.

He leaned in and she closed her eyes, his body thrumming with anticipation. His hand on her upper arm as he brought her close, her stomach fluttering, her body trembling. Her mouth was going dry and it felt like her heart was in her throat.

She wanted this.

Just once.

It only had to be once.

"*Querida*, I would very much like to kiss you," he murmured, brushing his knuckles gently over her cheek.

"I would very much like it if you did too," she responded, her voice shaking. It was against her better judgment. There was a rational side of her that was telling her to run, that this wasn't for her, but there was another part of her that was telling her that this was right.

This would be good.

This was worth it, even just for one moment in time.

Gus tipped her chin, so their gazes locked, and he bent down to press a light kiss against her mouth, sending a jolt of heat through her blood. Right down to the tips of her toes. It was almost too much, the heady sensation coursing through her.

She wanted more.

So much more.

She wrapped her arms around his neck, tangling her fingers in his hair at the nape of his neck to draw him in closer.

Deeper.

She was losing herself in this kiss.

She wanted to lose herself in this kiss.

For one night, she didn't want to be herself.

She broke off the kiss to get some air. He was still holding her close, but for her it was not close enough. She wanted more.

"Querida," he whispered, kissing her again.

"Shall we go back to the hotel?" she asked, her voice breaking.

"Are you sure?" he asked.

"Sí. Very much."

"Querida, I don't know… I can't promise you anything beyond tonight. You said so yourself, you're going home tomorrow and I leave to go back to my home in a couple of days. I can't give you a relationship, if that's what you're looking for."

"I'm not looking for a relationship, Gus. I just want tonight. That's all. So yes, I'm sure about going back and seeing where this takes us for tonight. I'm not looking for forever."

Gus nodded. They slipped on their shoes and she took his hand as they quickly walked back to the street to hail a cab and head back to their hotel.

She was nervous, but she wanted this more than anything.

Something to remember.

And she wanted it to be Gus.

Sharon seemed nervous.

He was nervous too and he didn't know why. He'd been with other women since his wife died and there was no emotional attachment to it, but with Sharon there was something else and he couldn't quite put his finger on it.

It made him want to be protective of her.

To comfort her and care for her, and those kinds of thoughts scared him. He wasn't going to let himself feel that way about anyone else. He wasn't going to open his heart and love someone else again.

He just couldn't do that.

Tonight though, tonight he wanted to be with her.

When she let him kiss her on the beach, it had been magical. Even just holding her lithe body in his arms and having her pressed against him had overwhelmed him. He wanted to lose himself in her arms, to drown himself in her kisses.

She was intoxicating.

He had been thrilled when she wanted to

come back to the hotel, but he was also nervous, because of the way she was affecting him.

Sharon didn't say much on the cab ride back to the hotel. Nor when they took the elevator, where he'd first laid eyes on her, to his room.

He opened the door and she stepped in.

Uncertain.

"Sharon, if you're not sure, we can just have a drink and talk."

She turned around quickly. "No. I want this. I have backed out of situations like this one too many times and I've regretted it after, always."

"Are you certain?" he asked.

Sharon sat down on the edge of the bed. "I am. I do want this, Gus, and I want it to be you."

"This isn't like some business transaction."

"I didn't expect so," Sharon stated matter-of-factly.

He ran his hand through his hair. "How about I pour us a drink? I have some wine."

"Okay."

Agustin grabbed two wineglasses from the minibar and opened the wine. It had been a gift from a business associate, but he couldn't take it back home with him to Argentina. He poured Sharon a glass and then himself one.

He sat down next to her.

"Thanks." She took the glass. Her hand was trembling.

"Don't be nervous," he said gently.

She smiled up at him. "I can't help it."

He touched her face gently. "You are sure about this?"

Sharon nodded. "Completely. I meant what I said on the beach, Gus. I don't expect anything after tonight. We'll go our separate ways. I just want to take this memory with me."

Then she reached out and touched his face. It was a light touch, gentle, and her skin felt like silk against his.

He took the empty wineglass from her and set them down.

There was a rational side of him that was screaming not to get involved, but when he looked into her eyes, he was lost.

He wanted to feel her against him.

He just wanted tonight too and he was honored that she chose him.

"We can stop any time you would like."

She smiled and then brushed her soft lips against his. "I appreciate that."

He cupped her face and kissed her deeply, drinking in her sweet taste.

Agustin knew he should stop.

He was in serious danger, but as her arms came around him and they sank against the mattress, he was a lost man.

What harm could come from one night?

CHAPTER THREE

*Ushuaia, Tierra del Fuego, Argentina,
five months later*

IT CAN'T BE.

She had only just arrived in Ushuaia. Yes, she had been feeling off since Spain, but how could she miss this?

Sharon sat down on the lid of the toilet, staring at the pregnancy test in her hand.

This was not part of the plan.

She was supposed to be here to take care of her grandmother. During her last job her aunt had called her and told her that her grandmother had fallen and broken her hip. Sharon knew she was the best one to go down there and see to her grandmother personally. That was what she planned to do.

A baby was not part of the plans.

Sharon didn't know how she was going to break the news to her grandmother.

The news she'd come here pregnant and unmarried.

Her grandmother was all alone in Ushuaia. There was no one to tend to her. Her aunt had her family, a husband in New York.

Sharon was single.

She'd given up her job, flown down to Tierra del Fuego, to the edge of Argentina to care for her abuela.

It was her pleasure.

Her abuela had always been there for her. Even though Sharon had grown up in the United States for the most part, she had been born in Ushuaia. Then her parents had moved to the US, following her aunt and uncle. Then her mother died and her father took off.

Sharon then divided her childhood between Ushuaia and where her aunt lived in the US. It was what gave Sharon her love of traveling.

In the first couple of days Sharon knew she'd have to stay here to take care of her abuela indefinitely. Her abuela's hip was not healing right and there were memory lapses.

Sharon still felt completely run-down, even after being here for two weeks.

Of course, a couple of weeks into taking care of her abuela Sharon got sick. She'd thought it had just been a bug, but the nausea and exhaustion had persisted. Then she'd noticed different things.

Other changes.

Changes she'd refused to believe were happening.

Until now.

Until that little stick had turned positive, letting her know she was indeed pregnant. She'd ignored all the symptoms for so long. Why had she done that? The first time in her life she decided to sleep with someone—using protection—she got pregnant.

"*Querida*, are you okay? You'll be late for work!" her abuela called.

"*Sí*, Abuela." Sharon sighed and continued to get ready in the small bathroom. She had most of the upstairs of the house to herself. Her grandmother couldn't get up the stairs still, but had the main floor set up. Soon her grandmother's day worker would be here.

She zoned out again, staring at the test.

"You'll be late. Remember, it's your first day, *querida*," her abuela reminded her again.

Right.

Her new job.

Sharon needed to work to pay for her abuela's care worker and to support them. It was going to be a great job at the most luxurious private plastic surgery clinic in Tierra del Fuego.

People from all over the world came to this clinic.

It was what had softened the blow of leaving her other job to come here.

Her abuela was right—she didn't want to be late for her first day.

She ran down the stairs and found her grandmother sitting up in her rocking chair and looking out the window.

"It's snowing," her abuela remarked, her voice laced with confusion. "Kind of early, isn't it?"

Sharon leaned over and looked out the window, groaning at the sight of snow. It was summer in the US. Her aunt would be heading to her cottage in the Finger Lakes. Sharon wished she was there right now, because here in Tierra del Fuego it was winter.

"Well, it is June first, Abuela," Sharon stated.

Abuela sighed. "Right. I forgot."

And Sharon knew her abuela was worried about the memory lapses.

Sharon kissed her on the top of her head. "It's okay to forget."

"You start work today at that fancy new clinic, yes?" Abuela asked, changing the subject.

"I do, but the clinic has been there for three years."

"Still new," her grandmother huffed. "When do you think you'll tell them you are pregnant?"

Sharon's blood ran cold. "What?"

"Oh, come on, Sharon. I'm old and I may have forgotten that winter started, but I know when someone is pregnant. I was a midwife for many years."

Sharon's voice shook. "I didn't even know… until now."

"You were too busy working and then moving here to care for me. Of course you didn't notice," her grandmother said, taking her hand. "I appreciate it, by the way. I love that you're here with me. I miss you when you're gone."

Sharon squatted and threw her arms around her grandmother, pulling her slight frame into her arms and holding her close. "I love you, Abuela."

"And I you, *querida*. I hope you know I'm thrilled with the idea of being a great-grandmother. I hope they will be born in Argentina. We have free health care here."

Sharon chuckled softly and got up. "I better get to work. Maria will be here soon to sit with you until I get back from work."

Her abuela nodded. "Have a good first day. I can't wait to hear all about it, and tonight you can tell me all about the father."

Sharon's stomach flipped as she pulled on her winter coat and headed out. There wasn't much to tell. It was an attractive man at a hotel during her last night in Barcelona.

Gus had been so wonderful to her.

It had been hard to leave him, but they'd made no promises.

She took a deep breath, the cold air filling her lungs. It was a short walk from her grandmother's home to the clinic. All downhill to the center of town.

Sharon was glad for the walk to clear her mind.

Snow was falling gently and the mountains in the distance had white caps, but there was a fog lingering over the city and the harbor.

It had been some time since she'd been back here in the place of her birth. She'd forgotten what it was like to live at the edge of the world. This had been a happy place. Her childhood had been full of tragedy, but coming here had been her happy times.

It was a great place to stay and working at a world-class clinic was a chance of a lifetime.

Maybe she could stay here.

There was a lot to process, and along with all the decisions she had to make, she also needed to somehow get hold of Gus and let him know she was pregnant. She may have been a one-night conquest to him, but he was the father and he had the right to know.

Her blood heated at the memory of their night together.

How he'd kissed her gently, how his strong hands had felt on her body, gently caressing her and making her melt. And when she told him it had been a long time for her, he had been so kind to ask if she was sure and then so patient with her during it all.

Making sure that she felt pleasure first.

And she had.

So much so, she couldn't believe that she had waited so long. It just had never felt quite right until that night in Barcelona. She was glad that it had been him, that she took a chance and listened to her gut that night.

She just hadn't been expecting a baby out of it, especially when they had used protection. Sharon shook the thought out of her mind. Today she had to give her all to her job. She had to support herself, her grandmother and now her baby.

It was something she was secretly thrilled with.

Even though it had taken her by surprise, she was thrilled with the ideas of being a mother. It was something she'd always wanted, but she never gave time to romance or relationships, so she'd thought it was something that was going to pass her by.

She reached down and cradled the small swell in her belly and smiled, even though the cold was biting at her bare cheeks.

She was happy. For the first time in a long time. It unnerved her how happy she was.

Sharon walked into the clinic and made her way to the employee locker room. She hung up her coat and purse in her assigned locker.

"Ah, so glad you're here, Sharon," Carmen, the head nurse, said brightly as she came into the room. She handed Sharon a set of scrubs. "For you."

"*Gracias,* Carmen." Sharon held the scrubs to her chest. "Where would you like me to start?"

"I'll have you work on the postoperative patients today. The surgeon, Dr. Varela, will be expecting your reports in an hour on their status."

Sharon's heart skipped a beat. There was so much she could learn here.

"Where can I find him?" Sharon asked, hoping her voice didn't crack with excitement.

Carmen smiled. "Agustin will be on the second floor. The offices are there. This is a nonsurgery day. Just postoperatives to take care of and the surgeons are running their clinics today, so they won't be down on the patient floor until later."

Sharon nodded. "Well, I better get changed."

"Find me at the nursing stating once you change. I have your key card and computer passcode so you can access patient files."

"*Gracias*, Carmen," Sharon said again.

Carmen smiled and left the room. Sharon changed into her scrubs. They were a little tight and she was annoyed because again she hadn't noticed the signs.

She made her way to the nursing station on the postoperative floor. Carmen gave her all she needed and she started her rounds.

She didn't need guidance. She'd worked as an operative nurse before. It was one of her favorite jobs.

Her last job had been at a family practice in the United States. This would be far more interesting.

Sharon grabbed the charts and made her

way to the first patient, a woman who'd had facial reconstruction after cancer.

She gently knocked on the door.

"Mrs. Sanchez, how are we today? I'm Nurse Misasi. You can call me Sharon."

Mrs. Sanchez stirred slightly, but didn't respond.

"Mrs. Sanchez?" Sharon leaned over. She gingerly touched Mrs. Sanchez's wrist. Her pulse was weak.

Mrs. Sanchez groaned. "Hurts."

"I'm sure," Sharon responded gently. "I'll get your meds."

Sharon took the patient's temperature.

"Hurts," Mrs. Sanchez moaned again.

"I know. Can I check your incisions?" Sharon asked.

Mrs. Sanchez groaned again and slightly nodded.

Sharon checked the incisions under the face wraps and they weren't healing as well as they should. The thermometer beeped and Mrs. Sanchez's temperature was elevated.

Sharon checked the readout of the monitor and then the chart. Mrs. Sanchez should be doing better and she couldn't help but wonder if the patient was allergic to something or was fighting an infection.

She was worried and knew that she was

going to have to page Mrs. Sanchez's surgeon for further instructions. This couldn't wait until he made his rounds later today.

"How is my patient this morning?"

Sharon heard the voice and her heart stopped as Dr. Agustin Varela entered Mrs. Sanchez's room. It was like a ghost from her past.

It was Gus.

It was someone she had been thinking about all morning. The man she had slept with in Barcelona. Gus was Dr. Agustin Varela. Her new boss was the father of her baby?

Agustin just stood there in shock as he stared at the new nurse, who was standing beside the bed of his patient Mrs. Sanchez. Carmen had told him when he'd called down that the new local nurse she hired had started today and was going to be doing the post-ops.

Usually, he hired his own staff, but he'd had to travel to Buenos Aires last week and bring his half sister, Sandrine, home from the school he'd tried to send her to, to get her away from her boyfriend Diego.

She had been living with his mother, but Sandrine was unhappy with the school, so he'd brought her home to Ushuaia.

He'd needed a new nurse, had no time to interview, so he'd left it to Carmen.

He trusted Carmen.

Agustin had been so worried about Mrs. Sanchez he hadn't wanted to leave it to chance with a nurse he wasn't familiar with. There was a reason his clinic was world-class: because he insisted on the best care for his patients.

This clinic was his life.

He hadn't been expecting his new nurse to be the woman he couldn't stop thinking about for the last five months.

Sharon.

He'd woken up to find her gone. They had made no promises, yet he was still hurt that she had disappeared like a thief in the night.

It stung, because that night had meant so much to him. For the first time since his wife died, he had felt a connection. A deep, meaningful moment of passion.

And since that night, he hadn't been able to get her out of his mind. When she'd left, it had hurt, but it had also been a relief, because the moment that he'd taken her in his arms he'd known that he had made a huge mistake.

She had ensnared him.

And when he brought her pleasure, she had broken through the ice that he had enshrined around his heart. He wanted more. It was easier to just try to forget her. She was leaving Spain.

For a week he tried to not think about her, but everywhere he looked her memory was lurking. Her kisses were still imprinted on his lips. So to try to put her out of his mind he threw himself into his work, running his clinic and trying to take care of Sandrine, since his father died last year and his stepmother had abandoned her. It was a lot.

The work, his father's messy estate, tracking down Sandrine's mother was keeping his mind off the woman who had left him.

Except in the lonely hours of the night when he would think of Sharon, wondering what happened to her.

He'd just had one of those awful sleepless nights, so he'd come in early to check on his post-op patients and there she was. Like she'd stepped out of his dreams, standing there in the aquamarine scrubs of the clinic, holding his patient's chart.

Her hair was done up in a bun again and she looked like she was staring at a ghost. He felt like he was too.

"How is she?" he asked, finding his voice. Agustin had a lot of questions to ask, but right now he had to focus on his patients.

"Her temperature is elevated and there's swelling at the incision site. The patient's blood pressure is elevated as well and she's complaining of pain, but I can see she's had her dose of pain medication only three hours ago."

Agustin took the chart from Sharon and stood next to her. It was hard to be so close to her. His pulse was thundering between his ears.

"I need a CBC on Mrs. Sanchez. It could be an infection," Agustin said, writing up the order.

Sharon nodded and took the chart back. "I will get the testing done straightaway."

"Have you managed to round on my other patients?" he asked.

Sharon shook her head. "This is just the start of my rounds."

Agustin nodded and checked over his patient. She was sleeping again and as he checked the incision site, he could see what Sharon was worried about. Mrs. Sanchez's incisions were red and swollen still. They shouldn't be this swollen.

"Well, I'm going to finish the rounds and you focus on the blood work of Mrs. Sanchez. I want that test done stat, and then report to me with the findings."

"Of course." She wasn't looking at him as she began to get the supplies ready for the blood test.

Agustin glanced back one more time and watched her moving around the patient's room. He couldn't believe that she was here. He'd thought Carmen had hired a local nurse.

Sharon had said she was from New York, but she'd also said her parents were from South America and she never did specify where. And he hadn't asked, because watching her on the beach at sunset, her parentage had been the furthest thing from his mind. It figured it had to be Argentina, and not even just Argentina, but Tierra del Fuego.

Agustin raked his hands through his hair and tried not to dwell on it. He finished his rounds with his other two surgical patients. Both of them were doing well and there was nothing to worry about. He would be able to discharge them in a couple of days.

By the time he finished with his last patient, it was almost time for his clinic to start and he saw Sharon coming quickly toward him. The aquamarine scrubs looked good on her, but she would look even better out of them.

He was annoyed with himself the moment he thought about her, naked in his arms, or how beautiful she had looked with the white cotton sheets wrapped around her sun-kissed body, her hair fanned out on the bed like a halo.

Almost like she was heaven-sent.

Get a grip on yourself.

"You have the lab results?" he asked, clearing his throat.

"Yes. Mrs. Sanchez has a staph infection. It's common," she replied.

Agustin didn't look at her, but stared at the results. "We need to change her antibiotics."

"Yes. I'll do that straightaway."

Agustin signed off on the orders so Sharon could start the medication. She looked a bit flushed and her cheeks were glowing, like she was sweating.

"Are you okay?" he asked.

"Fine," she said quickly.

"If you're sick…"

"I'm not sick."

"You don't look well. You look pale and tired."

Still gorgeous though.

Only he kept that thought to himself.

"I'm fine. Really," she replied stiffly, but he wasn't buying it. He could tell she was run-down or she was fighting something.

"If you have any kind of sickness you need

to tell me. I know it's your first day, but I can't have you putting the patients at risk."

Sharon frowned. "You really think me so foolish as to jeopardize patients, in particular surgical patients?"

"No, but then I don't know you."

Which was the truth. They hadn't talked much that night because neither of them had wanted to talk about work.

All they had was one incredible night together five months ago. Of course, they had both just wanted to have a moment of fun. They'd agreed, or he'd offered, that they wouldn't have deep conversations and that they'd just enjoy themselves.

And they had.

Just thinking about it again made his blood heat, his body thrum with desire, but then he had to remind himself that they weren't in Spain. He was her boss and she was his nurse, or rather the nurse that was working for him.

Sharon sighed. "I'm not sick. I know what's wrong with me."

"What's wrong with you then? Because I am concerned," he said firmly.

"I'm pregnant."

He could feel the blood drain from his face. "Pregnant?"

"Five months," she stated, under her breath and blushing.

"Five…" He trailed off as it hit him.

Sharon nodded. "I just found out today myself."

He took a step back and ran his hand through his hair.

He couldn't quite believe what he was hearing.

She was pregnant and the child was his.

"We used protection," he whispered.

"And you, as a physician, know that doesn't always work."

He wanted to talk to her more about this, but he was also terrified of the implications of it all. He had always wanted to be a father and ten years ago he came so close to that when he and Luisa had found out they were pregnant.

He'd had great aspirations of being a good father, unlike his own.

And that was all ruined.

He'd lost Luisa and he'd lost the child he was desperately excited for. The thought of having children seemed so out of reach to him, especially since he didn't ever plan on giving his heart to another woman.

Now here was Sharon. She was pregnant with his child and she was here in Ushuaia. A local. Like him.

"Dr. Varela, you're wanted in your office," the page came over the sound system.

"I better go," he said, dragging his hand through his hair. "We'll talk later."

"Of course," Sharon replied quietly. "I'll get the antibiotics set up for Mrs. Sanchez."

Agustin nodded. "Right. Keep me posted."

He turned around and made his way to the elevator. He had to put this on the back burner. He had his job to do and he could talk to her later and find out what she was doing in Ushuaia…and what they were going to do about their baby.

CHAPTER FOUR

Sharon had been slightly disappointed that Agustin hadn't said much of anything to her, but then again she couldn't blame him.

She was still in shock that the father of her baby was here in Ushuaia and not who she thought he was. Although they had never really talked about anything.

She'd known he was a doctor, but she'd had no idea that Gus was a plastic surgeon. She'd figured Gus was a cardiothoracic doctor or a cardiologist, something to do with hearts, because he had seemed to know about heart attacks.

And she'd suspected that Gus was from somewhere in South America, but they hadn't talked much about it. It just figured he was from Argentina, from Ushuaia, and he probably knew her abuela too.

This felt like some weird comedy of coincidences.

Gus had been a sexy stranger she had flirted with all week at the conference. Her one-night stand. That had been it.

Now he was her boss? Dr. Agustin Varela.

She was relieved when he was called away to the clinic. He'd mumbled they would talk later and left.

That was fine by her.

She didn't want a relationship. That hadn't changed.

If he wanted to be in the baby's life then great, but she wouldn't allow him to abandon her child and break its heart.

You need to focus on your work.

She shook out all those foggy thoughts.

She was a professional and she had a job to do. She couldn't think about the fact her boss was the father of her unborn baby or that he was her one-night stand.

The man who had awakened passion deep inside her.

Get a hold of yourself, Sharon.

She couldn't let thoughts of that night intrude on her work. At least he now knew about the baby and she wouldn't have to worry about figuring out how to get hold of Gus to let him know that he was going to be a father.

At least that was taken care of.

Sharon made sure Mrs. Sanchez got the antibiotics she needed and started a central line. She continued her duties for the day and finished her charting.

Agustin hadn't come back to the postoperative floor, not that she could blame him. She was sure it had been a shock to see her here, his new nurse, who was pregnant with his child while he had a world-class practice to run.

When they had dinner in Barcelona at that café he'd told her that he put his all into work as well. That was the only thing he'd divulged.

It was one of the things that she admired about him.

He had the same passion for his career as she did. Though she hadn't known who he was at the time.

Work was her life too.

She understood that.

She respected that.

Except work would soon have to take a back seat to the little life growing inside her. She reached down and touched her abdomen. Overwhelmed was an understatement for how she felt right now.

There was a lot to do.

One step at a time, Sharon.

That was how she'd gotten through her mother's death and her father's abandonment.

She took her life one step at a time.

She took a deep, calming breath and finished her shift. The night nurses to care for the postoperative patients came in and she handed over the charts gladly. She went to the locker room and changed back into her street clothes.

The night nurses said it was snowing hard and the temperature was dropping. She was glad for the warm parka that she had. She just wanted to get home.

As she walked outside, she saw Agustin, under a streetlamp leaning against a black sedan, bundled up against the cold snow of June.

"Hey," she said, surprised. "You look like you're freezing."

"I am. I drive so I don't need a parka like you are smartly wearing."

Sharon chuckled. "I don't have a car, so I walk."

"Can I give you a ride home, or perhaps we can go somewhere to talk?"

Sharon glanced at her watch. She had to relieve Maria and her grandmother couldn't be alone for too long just yet. "I'm sorry, I can't. I really need to get home."

"Don't you think we should talk?" Agustin asked.

"I do, but I have to get back home and relieve my abuela's care worker."

He looked confused. "I thought you were from the States?"

"I am, but also here. My grandmother lives here. I was born here." Sharon glanced at her watch again. "I want to talk about what's happening. I do feel bad for springing it on you, but you had the right to know, it's just I really have to get back home."

"Fair enough. I'll drive you."

"You don't have to," she argued. Although, her feet were aching and she wouldn't mind the ride home.

"No. Let me, and then maybe tomorrow at lunch we can go somewhere and talk?"

"I'd like that."

Agustin nodded and opened the door to his car. She slid into the passenger seat. He got into the driver seat. "So where am I driving you to?"

"Near Los Guindos. It's not far from here."

A strange look crossed his face. Just a brief flicker of confusion and shock.

"I know that neighborhood well," he said stiffly.

She didn't know what to say. A tense silence fell between them.

"So, I thought you were in Spain?" she asked, breaking the silence.

"Spain is not my home. Ushuaia is," he stated. "I was there for the conference. As were you if I recall."

"Yes. I didn't actually ask where you were from, did I?"

"No. We didn't really deep dive into too much, other than you were from New York."

"So we're both from Ushuaia and met in Spain?" She chuckled. "Seems a bit…odd. Way too coincidental."

"Yes. Very odd," he agreed and then he had to laugh. "Like a bad comedy."

"Yes. I suppose. I did think the same thing." She chuckled nervously.

"Well, that's a relief you were thinking it was odd too."

An awkward silence fell between them. Sharon stared down at her hands. This was certainly not how she'd pictured telling Gus, or rather Agustin. It was easier this morning to think of him still in Spain.

On the beach.

In that hotel room.

In her arms.

Heat crept up her neck. She had to get control of those thoughts. They weren't in Barcelona now. A lot had changed and she had to remember that.

In fact, there was a part of her that didn't think he would care too much that she was pregnant, and that would be fine by her, but she wasn't not going to tell him and keep her pregnancy a secret. That wasn't her jam.

It certainly had never been in her wildest dreams that he would be her boss and that she would be working side by side with him. Why did he have to be from Ushuaia too? Argentina was big, but she rarely ran into people who were from Ushuaia. Actually, most people had never even heard of Tierra del Fuego.

Of course, the one man she decided to spend a night with the one time she let down her guard and decided to taste that forbidden fruit of passion happened to be a man from Ushuaia, and he happened to be a surgeon. And now they were working together.

Her grandmother was going to think this was funny.

Thankfully, it wasn't a long ride to her grandmother's home. The moment they pulled up on the street, Maria was pacing outside, wringing her hands.

"Oh, no," Sharon murmured.

"A relative?" Agustin asked.

"No, it's my abuela's care worker."

Agustin parked the car and Sharon got out and made her way to Maria.

"Maria, what's wrong?" Sharon asked, fearing the worst.

"It's your abuela. She's being stubborn," Maria said hastily.

Sharon groaned inwardly. "She can be. Tell me what happened?"

"She fell, hit her head and is insisting it's a scratch, but it's bleeding. It's her forehead. I doubt she has a concussion, but you know how much head wounds bleed. She took away my phone, didn't want me to call you and bother you since you were on your way home, and I can't call an ambulance. Then she didn't remember me. I tried the neighbors and no one is home. The teenager who lives there is still at school."

"She'd better be at school," Agustin said stiffly. "I'm your neighbor and that teenager is my half sister."

Sharon was shocked. "You're my neighbor?"

"Apparently, though I've been in Buenos Aires for the last two weeks."

Sharon pinched the bridge of her nose. This was just getting more and more complicated. She took a deep breath. "Where is my abuela now, Maria?"

"She locked herself in her room. The fall literally just happened," Maria said.

"I'll retrieve your phone and then I'll take care of her so you can go home and try to relax this evening."

Maria chuckled. *"Gracias."*

Sharon walked into the house and made her way to her grandmother's room. She knocked on the door. "Abuela, open up."

"Querida?"

"Yes. I need Maria's phone back so she can go home."

"I don't need to see a doctor!" her abuela shouted.

Sharon sighed, not sure what had come over her grandmother, and of course it had to happen right now, with Agustin outside and on the day she found out she was pregnant. She heard the click of the lock turning.

The door opened and Abuela held out Maria's phone, just through the crack of the door. Sharon took the phone and ran it outside to Maria.

Maria thanked Sharon and said she would be back tomorrow at the same time, so Sharon was relieved that her abuela hadn't scared off her care worker.

Sharon headed back inside and saw that her abuela had opened the door, was sitting on her bed, and that Agustin was kneeling down in front of her, examining her head wound. Sharon was confused.

When did he come inside?

Her grandmother looked over at her. "Sharon, this is Agustin Varela. His father was my neighbor and he's our neighbor too!"

"I am aware," Sharon said stiffly.

Agustin didn't smile, but then again if his father had recently died then she could understand that he was grieving still. She didn't know when Mr. Varela died. She'd only been here a couple of weeks.

And clueless to a lot of things.

Sharon sat down next to her grandmother and took her hand. "How bad is it?"

Agustin looked up at her. "Superficial, but it's still bleeding. She would benefit from some stitches. We should get her to the hospital."

"No," her abuela stated. "I won't go there. I don't need to."

Sharon sighed. "Abuela…"

"No." Her grandmother took back her hand and sat up straighter, crossing her arms, but Sharon knew she was becoming agitated.

Agustin stood. "I could do it. We could take her to the clinic and I can stitch her up there."

"You don't have to do that," Sharon said gently.

"It's no problem. It's the least I could do for the woman who delivered me thirty-five years ago." He winked at her grandmother.

Abuela smiled. "Yes. I did deliver you, and I delivered your father, Theo, too."

Agustin's smile, which had extended to a twinkle in his eyes, changed at the mention of his father. "Did you deliver my half sister, Sandrine?"

"No. Sandrine's mother insisted on a fancy clinic in Buenos Aires," her abuela said. "I never liked that woman and I liked her less after she left her daughter. I am sorry about that, Agustin. I'm glad you take care of her."

Agustin nodded curtly. "Well, let's get you to the clinic."

He left the room to wash his hands in the small bathroom on the main floor. He came back with fresh dressings and Sharon took them from him. He barely looked at her. It was almost like he was ashamed that she knew his secrets.

Not that she could blame him.

Abuela wasn't a woman to keep secrets. Especially lately as she aged and her memory went. She was grateful for Agustin's gentle hand. She made sure her grandmother's wound was covered and then helped her abuela get up and put on her outside gear.

Agustin held the door for them and then took Abuela's arm on the other side, and the both them walked her to the front seat of the car, settling her in for the short drive to the clinic. Abuela was grinning the whole time they drove to the private clinic.

Sharon wasn't sure what this new fear of the hospital was, but at least her grandmother would have that wound stitched up and taken care of without too much of a fight. It was worrying her, this change in her grandmother's behavior.

Agustin parked in his parking spot, which was near the door of the clinic. He went inside and got a wheelchair as Sharon helped her grandmother out of his car.

"I don't need that," Abuela stated. "I can walk."

"I insist," Agustin said firmly. "Clinic procedures."

Abuela nodded and sat down.

Sharon followed Agustin numbly, feeling like she was out of place. Agustin took the elevator straight to clinic floor, which was empty at this time of night. He wheeled Abuela into one of the exam rooms, which had a nice bed and was completely fitted out.

Agustin helped her grandmother up onto the bed and then took off his coat. Sharon slipped off her coat.

"I want to help," she said. "I mean, this is my job."

Agustin smiled and nodded. "Well, if you can get a suturing kit from the supply closet, I'll prep the anesthetic."

"I can do that." Sharon wanted to keep herself busy and not think about the fact that Agustin suddenly seemed to be inserted into her life. More than she ever imagined him to be. Just this morning he was someone who was far away and she was trying to figure out how to get hold of him to let him know that she was pregnant.

Now here he was, her boss, her grandmother's neighbor, and he was about to suture up her grandmother's head.

Sharon headed back into the exam room.

Agustin was talking to her grandmother and making her laugh.

"Here's the suture kit," Sharon announced.

He turned and smiled. That dazzling, charming smile that had won her over five months ago. "Great. Thanks."

"Can I do anything else?" Sharon asked.

"Nope. Just sit with your grandmother," Agustin said as he readied his tools. "I numbed her up and gave her something to calm her down. She may have a nap here."

"I'm very comfy," her abuela murmured sleepily.

"It's okay, you can nap here for a bit. Sandrine will be fine on her own, as she tells me often," Agustin groused.

Her grandmother closed her eyes.

Sharon sat there in a chair next to her grandmother, feeling absolutely useless.

"So that's your sister. I've met her. She's nice."

"Yes. Her name is Sandrine." Agustin continued to work on her grandmother's head.

"I know," Sharon said softly. "She never mentioned you."

"I'm not surprised. She's sixteen and keeps to herself. For the most part."

"You mean for a teenager?" she asked.

"Precisely. I had her at a good school in Buenos Aires for a time, but she loathed it. I suspect she's still mad at me."

"When did your father die?"

Agustin tensed. "A year ago."

"Where's Sandrine's mother?"

Agustin shrugged. "My stepmother? No idea. She left, abandoned Sandrine to my care."

Sharon's heart sank.

She knew that scenario well.

"Querida," her aunt Sophia had said, choking. There'd been tears in her eyes.

Sharon had stood there, staring up at the police officers.

There'd been so many people in her home. She'd clutched her doll tight to her chest. It was like a shield. That was what she'd been telling herself for days, since she'd woken up and realized her father had gone.

She'd kept her dolly close to her as she'd eaten what she could, because she hadn't been allowed to use the stove.

I think she's in shock, ma'am. We'll have her taken to the children's hospital to check, a police officer had said.

Her aunt had nodded, kneeling down next to her. *Querida?*

Is Daddy dead? she'd asked, her voice hollow, because now she was recalling when her mother had died. All the police and people had been there then too.

No, her aunt had said, smiling. *No, we don't know where he is, but we're going to take you to the hospital and you can come sleep over at my house. Would you like that?*

Sharon had nodded. *But Daddy said to wait. He always told me to wait. Should I still wait?*

No, querida. *Come.* Her aunt had held out her hand. *Come.*

Sharon shook those memories away, her throat thickening. She hated that that memory had been triggered. It was something she kept locked away tightly. She didn't want it to intrude on her life.

"Well, to be honest, I did think it was rotten she left Sandrine alone. I had no idea. Sandrine said she was used to being on her own for bouts of time…"

Agustin sighed. "Yes. Well, I didn't have much to do with my father and didn't know much about my half sister. My mother in Buenos Aires found out and called me. Sandrine reached out to her when her mother didn't return. Thankfully, I was here and not traveling at the time."

Sharon's heart melted. It was clear Agustin had no feelings toward his late father or his stepmother, but he cared enough about his half sister to put his life on hold and come and do the right thing. Sharon was all too familiar with having hard feelings toward one's father. Hers had left. Agustin was a decent, honorable man who was here for his sister who'd been abandoned after a parent's death. Much like Sharon had been left.

She had been younger than Sandrine and

thankfully had her aunt and her abuela to step in. Her aunt had been in the States and her abuela had flown up from Tierra del Fuego to work out an arrangement to take care of her.

Sharon had always appreciated that.

Sandrine had been alone.

"There. Your abuela will be right as rain." Agustin finished putting the dressing on.

"Thank you. I don't know what came over her." Sharon sighed. "She's had small brief episodes since her fall, but she's never taken to stealing someone's phone, locking herself away and refusing medical help."

"She didn't refuse me." He grinned, winking.

Sharon chuckled. "True."

Agustin was hard to resist. She should know.

"I'm glad to help." Agustin stood and disposed of the used suture kit, removed his gloves and washed his hands.

"How long will she sleep do you think? I'm asking because I have no idea what you've given her."

"Maybe an hour or two and then I'll take you home. I told Sandrine I'd be home late. She responded with 'k.' Not 'okay' or 'all right,' but 'k.' Just the letter."

Sharon smiled. "She sounds like my preteen cousins."

"Shall we grab something to eat? Your

grandmother will be fine. I can get us a couple of takeaways from the food cart outside?"

She should say no, but she was starving. "I would like that."

He nodded. "I'll be back in a few."

He left the exam room and Sharon leaned back in her chair. It had been a long day. She wished she was at home in bed. That had been her plan once she settled her grandmother for the night. She was going to have a bath, get into comfy pajamas and watch television.

This was the most surreal first day of her life.

There was a part of her that wanted to quit because working with Agustin would be awkward and weird, but she was no quitter and she needed to support herself and her abuela.

She was staying in Ushuaia for the foreseeable future to give her baby stability. This was a great job. One she could come to love. She'd make this work with Agustin. They were both adults.

This would have to work.

There was no other choice.

Agustin's head was pounding slightly and he was distracted as he bought a couple of meals from the cart outside the clinic.

Of course, he'd been completely distracted

since he discovered his new nurse was Sharon and she told him she was pregnant. It secretly thrilled him, but also unnerved him too. They had used protection, though he knew that wasn't always a sure thing.

He had given up hope of ever becoming a father. Especially after what happened to Luisa and their unborn child. It nearly ended him when he lost them, so he'd made peace with the idea that he'd be alone for the rest of his life because it was easier this way.

Easier to eke out the rest of his existence alone.

No feeling.

No pain.

And then Sharon came along.

Pregnant and apparently his neighbor!

Sharon said she had been here two weeks, but he had been in Buenos Aires and then trying to conduct other business when he brought Sandrine back to Ushuaïa. He hadn't noticed Sharon was right under his nose this whole time.

Why don't you like the school? Agustin had asked.

Because I'm lonely. Your mother, she's amazing and I've always loved her. She's never treated me bad for what my mother did, but it's not the same. It's not home.

Agustin had sighed. *You mean because Diego isn't there.*

Sandrine had looked sad. *You never listen. You never pay attention.*

Fine. You can come home, but I have lots of work coming up.

Right. Work.

His life revolved around work so the grief of losing Luisa wouldn't eat away at him. Work was a balm to soothe his shattered heart. Sex was a distraction move.

Until Sharon.

It boggled his mind how their paths seemed to be crossing.

When they had their night together neither of them shared too much about themselves. They'd both agreed to that because neither one of them could promise more than one night.

Now, within a span of a day, they both knew far too much about each other.

Dios, her abuela delivered him and his father!

So much for a one-night stand.

Now there were many subtle layers tying them together. Fate was entwining their paths and he wasn't sure why. All he could do was laugh about it, although maybe he would laugh about it later. Right now, he wasn't thinking about that—he was thinking about his heart.

He made his way back upstairs and found Sharon dozing in the chair next to her grandmother.

Sharon looked so peaceful and tired. His gaze traveled over her, remembering with exquisite detail her body under his hands, and then he saw the slight swell, just ever so slight, and it looked like she was cradling it.

It made his heart skip a beat.

She's off-limits. She works for you.

And he had to keep reminding himself of that.

Both of them had made it clear they didn't want a relationship, but they could both be involved with their child's life. He could see his baby every day.

What if she doesn't plan to stay here? What if she went back to the States?

Agustin didn't like that niggly thought at the back of his mind.

Then the ever-darker thoughts of fate snatching this child away from him too.

Please don't tell me, Agustin had said, choking back the tears.

The trauma surgeon's face had been somber and Agustin had been pulled into one of those rooms. A room where they gave patients' families bad news. A place that was private and hidden away from everyone else.

Please... Agustin had begged, hoping that if he kept saying please then the truth wouldn't come out, but he knew it to be true.

He could tell.

Luisa was gone.

His child was gone.

I'm sorry, Dr. Varela, the surgeon had said. *They were brought to the emergency room without vital signs. We tried everything, but she was gone.*

Agustin had fallen to his knees and wept.

Everything had been taken away from him.

Everything had gone and was broken...

Sharon stirred and opened her eyes. "Oh, you're back."

He plastered a fake smile on his face, to keep back the sadness that was threatening to overtake him. "Come to my office. It's just next door. We can eat, talk and leave the door open to keep an eye on your abuela."

Sharon nodded and followed him to his office.

"What would you like?" he asked. "I got empanadas and asado. I bought your abuela provoleta because I remember hers at community picnics."

"I'll have asado please. It's my favorite."

Agustin nodded and handed her the Styrofoam takeaway box.

"I guess I am getting my way," he said teasingly, sitting down and digging into his food, though he couldn't really taste it.

"How is that?" she asked.

He smiled. "Dinner and a chance to talk."

Her dark brown eyes twinkled. "I suppose so."

"I am glad to talk, but I would've preferred not to have your abuela fall in order to have this chance to talk to you tonight."

"I know."

"So you've been back here for two weeks?"

Sharon nodded. "Yes. I was taking care of my abuela. I spent a lot of time getting her out of the hospital and settling her back at home. I upended my whole life to come here."

"You weren't working before?" he asked. "Because this was your first day I believe."

"No. I quit my previous job when I understood the nature of my abuela's fall and the help she'd require. I'm here now."

"Permanently?" he asked, trying to feel her out.

"For now," she said.

Agustin didn't like her vague answers.

"For now" wasn't a definite yes. It was not cut-and-dried.

"You said you only found out today?"

"Yes." She groaned. "I've been so busy with

my grandmother, the move and finding work I ignored the signs."

"So I am assuming you haven't got an obstetrician yet?"

"No. This is a lot of questions," she said.

He grinned. "Sorry, but we're beyond the point of mystery now that you carry our child."

Sharon nodded. "True."

Her grandmother moaned and called out for Sharon, so she went to her while Agustin cleaned up. He poked his head into the exam room. "I'll get the wheelchair and we'll take your grandmother home."

"Thank you. For dinner and your help tonight," Sharon said quietly. "I really appreciate it… Agustin. Or should I call you Gus?" she asked, a smile playing on her lips.

"Agustin or Gus, doesn't matter."

A blush tinged her cheeks. "I like Agustin." She said it shyly and it warmed his heart. What was it about her?

Be careful.

And he had to be. He couldn't take another heartbreak.

He just nodded and closed the door between his office and the exam room. He had a lot to figure out. Not only with Sharon but with Sandrine and her insistence that she be with that boy Diego. It was all so complicated.

Life had been easier when he was alone, working to build his clinic.

When he didn't have to think about grief or loss or family.

Things he'd accepted he'd never risk again after Luisa died.

It had been so much better then.

Hadn't it?

CHAPTER FIVE

THERE WAS A crick in his neck when he woke up and he was confused as to where he was. Then it all came rushing back to him as his eyes adjusted to the dim light. He was at home, but he had crashed on the couch. A bunch of work was scattered around him.

After he had taken Sharon and her abuela home, he'd gone home to see Sandrine. Only she hadn't been there.

She'd been out with that boy again.

When Sandrine got home she'd marched straight upstairs. There was no point in yelling at her, but he was annoyed all the same.

Agustin sat up slowly and stretched. He hadn't realized that he'd fallen asleep on the couch. He hadn't realized how tired he had been. He was used to working late into the night.

"You're awake. I was going to poke you

with a pair of tongs to see if you were still alive," Sandrine said from the kitchen.

"Thanks," he groused.

"Where were you last evening?"

He ran his fingers through his hair. "I know where you were."

She shrugged. "Look, you're never around. Always working. I need to live my own life."

"You're sixteen."

"So? I was fifteen when Dad died and you came here. Nothing has changed. I can fend for myself."

Agustin felt bad.

"So where were you?" she asked.

"My new nurse, she lives next door. Her abuela fell and…"

"Theresa fell?" Sandrine gasped.

"You know her well?"

Sandrine made a face. "Everyone around here does. She's the neighborhood grandma."

He remembered that then.

He'd buried those memories, but it all came flooding back to him.

After his father left his mother when he was in university in Buenos Aires, he never came back to Ushuaia. He preferred his mother's home. He distanced himself from his father, although his father tried to reach out.

When Luisa died, Agustin came back to

Ushuaia, as Buenos Aires held painful memories of her, but he avoided his childhood home and his father as much as he could. Now that his father had died, he was back living at home with his half sister.

There were even some brief memories of Sharon, although he was a teenager when she was a young child.

How long had Sharon and his life been intersecting?

Agustin shook that thought away.

"You ready for school?" Agustin asked groggily.

"Yep." Sandrine stared at her phone.

Then he remembered all his suits were at the dry cleaner since he'd been in Buenos Aires these last two weeks. He'd planned to pick them up, but got sidetracked yesterday.

"You didn't happen to go to the dry cleaner?" Agustin asked.

"Nope," Sandrine replied.

He groaned. "Great."

He really needed to hire a maid. Maybe then he could keep better tabs on Sandrine and that boy.

"You know, Dad's room is full of suits," she remarked.

His stomach turned. He and his father had never had the best relationship. His father had left his mother for a younger woman, Sandrine's mother.

When his father died Sandrine's mother vanished and Agustin stepped up.

It was weird moving back into his childhood home, but it had been left to him.

Agustin wondered if Sandrine's mother would ever come back, but it was a touchy subject.

It was hard being surrounded by good memories of his parents, but also painful ones of their divorce and his estrangement from his father.

He lived here for Sandrine's sake, but he didn't like being here.

"I'm going to clean up."

Her lips quirked in a small, brief smile. "'Kay."

Agustin groaned and made his way to the bathroom. He was pretty sure that he could find a dress shirt that would be acceptable for work and then he'd get the dry cleaning.

He opened the door to his father's room.

Even though it had been a year since his father died he could still smell him in that room, which was strange. He made his way to the closet and found a blue dress shirt that would match his trousers and suit jacket.

He peeled off his clothes and headed into

his father's en suite bathroom, turning on the hot water. He was hoping a nice hot shower would let him think. He'd thought his whole life was figured out.

He just couldn't ever forgive his father.

He finished his shower, dried off and put on the fresh shirt and the rest of his suit. He picked one of his father's ties and headed out for the day. Sandrine had left for school. He had a few appointments today and some in-patient surgeries that he was hoping Sharon could assist him with.

As he made his way outside, he met Sharon heading out the door. She looked adorable bundled up in her winter wear. It made him smile.

"Good morning," he said brightly. "Would you like a ride?"

"It's not a long walk and I need the exercise. You could walk with me," she said teasingly.

He groaned inwardly. "Fine, but you're just going to make me walk back here again and then I have to drive back into town to get my dry cleaning."

"You don't have a personal assistant or a maid for that?" she asked, surprised.

"I am an adult. I'm quite capable," he groused.

"Except you're still not dressed for winter."
She smiled.

He glanced down. "No, but as I said I drive everywhere."

"Still no excuse. So are you walking with me or driving?"

"I'll walk. I guess I can take a cab later." He shoved his hands into his pockets.

He had no idea how she'd convinced him to walk. He was grumbling about his decision but he liked to be around her. That hadn't changed since Barcelona.

He'd liked being with her then, the beautiful stranger, and now he was slightly protective over the fact she was carrying their child.

"I remember you, you know," he said, breaking the silence.

"Well, I hope so," she teased.

"I mean from years ago. Your abuela, she was sort of a neighborhood grandma. And I remember this small, shy girl with pink ribbons in her hair. I was a teen then, but I remember your abuela's American granddaughter."

Sharon laughed. "Yes. The pink ribbons. I'm sorry I don't remember you."

"I am a lot older." He winked at her.

"Not that much," she said quickly. "My summers here were a bit of a blur."

There was a hint of sadness in her voice. He

wanted to ask her why, when she pulled out a candy from her pocket, unwrapped it and popped it into her mouth.

"Are you okay?" he asked.

"Just a bit of morning sickness."

"You're at twenty weeks though. You should be over it." Although, this summation was completely based on his brief time as an intern when he had to work different specialties to become and surgeon and the small window of time Luisa had been forcing him to read all those pregnancy books.

He really had no idea. And Luisa had never made it that far into her pregnancy.

He'd been a young surgeon then too, just starting out, and wasn't completely engaged with Luisa's pregnancy.

He'd worked to support Luisa and the baby. That had come first.

Always.

And the guilt of that still tore at his wounded heart.

"Tell that to the fetus," Sharon groused.

"You really need to book an ultrasound and an appointment with an OB/GYN or a midwife. Someone who specializes in prenatal care. You're halfway there and haven't seen anyone."

"I know. I am so frustrated with myself."

"Why?" he asked quizzically.

"I didn't see the signs. I even missed the quickening." Her voice caught in her throat and he hoped that she wasn't going to cry. He wasn't sure how he could deal with her heart breaking.

"You can feel the baby now?" he asked, hoping his excitement didn't show through. He wanted to give her space, yet the thought of the little life growing inside her excited him just as much as it terrified him.

His child. A second chance.

Words he never thought he'd ever think or say since the crash and losing Luisa and their unborn baby. He fought the urge to reach out and touch her belly, to see if he could feel his child moving, but he resisted.

"So that's why you have the candy then?" he asked.

"Ginger candy. It's not perfect, but it helps with the nausea," she mumbled. "Truth be told, I really detest ginger…"

They continued their walk to the clinic, not saying anything, but in that moment they didn't need to. It was easy walking with her. He didn't mind the cold so much when he was with her.

It felt right.

Which was alarming.

"Have you worked in an operating room before?" Agustin asked. "I have seen your curriculum vitae, but I can't recall if you have scrub nurse experience. I just remember you mentioning triage."

"Yes. I'm quite adept at all forms of nursing and I really do enjoy the aspects of being a scrub nurse."

He smiled at the way she talked about her work. She was so formal and so logical a lot of the time, but her eyes would light up when she talked about work. She was clearly passionate about it.

He wondered if her formality was a way that she kept people out, kept people at bay, and he wondered what she was holding back from him.

Why does it matter? She's not yours, so it's not your business.

He was holding back too.

He didn't want to let her in. So why did he want *her* to let *him* in?

What was happening to him?

"I have some outpatient surgeries today. Since you're on my rotation I would like your assistance in the operating room."

"Are you testing my abilities?" she said teasingly.

He grinned. "Perhaps. Just a bit."

"Well, I will rise to the challenge gladly." And she nodded her head for good measure, the parka hood sliding forward a bit.

"Good." Agustin unlocked the door to the clinic and held it open for her. "I will meet you in my office in twenty minutes and then we can go over what's expected today and the surgical procedures."

"That sounds good."

She pushed back the hood and he caught the scent of her subtle shampoo. A simple, clean smell he remembered vividly.

How he'd longed to run his fingers through her hair that night they were together, and he could recall achingly still how it felt.

An errant strand of her hair blew around her face and without thinking he reached down and brushed it away.

Her skin was as soft as he remembered. Her cheeks flushed.

"Thanks," she said, tucking the strand behind her ear. "So twenty minutes?"

She was obviously changing the subject, which was for the best.

"Yes."

"See you then, Agustin." She didn't look at him as she stepped inside.

Agustin took a deep breath and followed Sharon inside. They were both trying to keep this professional, but he couldn't help but feel this unwanted attachment to her and her well-being growing inside him.

Try as he might, he couldn't deny that night in Barcelona had been more than a regular one-night stand. More than he wanted to admit.

Sharon was trying to keep the nausea at bay. She wasn't sure if it was stress after the events of yesterday or what was going on. One of the things she loved in nursing was working the operating room. She loved getting those jobs. She found it comforting and challenging.

Right now, the smells were getting to her. She was able to get the patients prepped. A lot of the outpatient procedures today had been things like the removal of moles or skin tags or injections of some sort.

This was the final procedure of the day and it was one that required anesthetic and working in the operating room. She wasn't sure if it was the cautery or something else that was causing her to feel awful. She stood next to Agustin as he worked on the liposuction of the patient. The sound of the machines was bothering her and making her ears ring.

She tried to ignore that sensation and focused on the procedure steps—by doing that she could keep all the stomach churning at bay and do her job.

She was determined to keep things professional but it was hard to do that when she was feeling ill and thinking about Agustin brushing away a strand of her hair.

It wasn't turning her stomach, but it made her stomach flutter in a different way.

In a way that was not professional at all.

She liked that he seemed to care for her and the baby, yet he was holding something back and it terrified her.

What if he walked away like her own father had?

It made her anxious to think of her baby feeling the pain of abandonment.

All of this just added to her nausea, her anxiety.

Sharon rolled her shoulders and ignored those racing thoughts. Focusing on work was what she'd done yesterday when he'd sutured up her abuela. He was excellent at suturing and she admired his handiwork.

"Sharon, can you hold this clamp for me?" Agustin asked.

"Of course." She stepped in and took the clamp, and, as she did so, their gazes locked and her pulse began to race.

The anesthesiologist cleared his throat and she cursed inwardly. It was the last thing she wanted, for everyone to suspect there was something going on between her and Agustin. She had to be careful. No one could know.

That time had meant nothing.

Or did it?

Sharon ignored that little voice. Sure, he had been her first time and it had been so magical and yes, she was carrying his baby, but she couldn't get attached to him.

People left. Hearts were broken when you allowed yourself to get attached to people. Even Agustin knew that with his own parents. There was no such thing as love. Except now, here with him, she had all these warm feelings.

Watching him work, getting to know him. Watching him with her abuela. She wasn't sure what was happening to her. She knew one thing: she didn't particularly like it.

Sharon closed her eyes as another wave of nausea washed over her.

She was able to gain some control to continue with her work.

"There. I think we can close up," Agustin announced. "Sutures please."

He held out his hand and Sharon retrieved

what he needed to close up the small incision from the liposuction.

The scent of the operating room was getting to her again, but she focused on all the tasks as the patient was closed and taken to the postanesthetic unit. She gripped the edge of the instrument table, which she would have to take to be sterilized.

"You did well," Agustin remarked. "I'm pleased with your abilities."

She turned her head slowly to see him at the operating room computer, sitting on a swivel stool and typing up his operative notes.

"Thanks," she said weakly, feeling very hot even though the operating room was not a warm environment.

"I definitely would have you work in the operating room with me again."

"I would…" She tried to focus on a source of something, anything that would keep her grounded, but her vision was narrowing at the sides.

"Sharon?" Agustin called out, his voice like an echo.

She was feeling very overheated as her source of light faded away and her knees gave out.

The last thing she saw was Agustin leaping up, his arms outstretched as the world went black.

* * *

"Sharon?" It was Agustin's voice. He was pressing a cold something to her forehead and it felt good.

"Hmm?"

"You fainted."

She opened her eyes and looked up at him. "I...what?"

"You fainted," he said gently. "I've called for an OB/GYN friend of one of my colleagues."

Sharon groaned. "So they all know I'm pregnant."

"Who are 'they'?" he asked.

"The others in here," she moaned.

"What would you have me do? Yes, you're pregnant. Even you can see the logic in my decision to call for someone who is more skilled than I am!"

She groaned again. Her head was hurting. Agustin was right, but it was no good him making sense right now, which sort of irritated her. She was frustrated the secret was out, but really how much longer had she thought she was going to be able to keep it? Others would soon notice.

"Can you sit up?" he asked.

"I think so," she murmured.

Agustin's arms came around her and he

gently helped her up off the operating room floor. "Let's get you to an exam room for Dr. Perez to check that everything's okay."

Sharon nodded and let Agustin hold her, but she was still wobbly on her feet and couldn't stand upright. Before she could say anything or even protest, Agustin scooped her up in his arms and carried her from the operating room.

She was mortified, but also felt safe.

Being in his arms brought back the memory of their night together, making her blood heat and her nipples tighten under her scrubs, and she really hoped she wasn't blushing. She would hate for him to see how she still reacted to his touch.

She was trying to keep things professional. It was hard to do when your boss was carrying you through the halls though.

Agustin carried her into an open exam room and gently set her down on the exam table, the paper crinkling.

"There. I'll stay with you if that's okay?" he asked.

"You don't have to," she said. "Remember, there is nothing between us."

A strange expression crossed his face for just a moment. "I know, but it's my baby and I want to be involved."

Of course. The baby.

Good.

She was glad he was focused on that and not her.

She didn't want a relationship.

Don't you?

She ignored that voice.

"Okay, yes. Please stay."

There was nothing about this whole situation that would ever be permanent. She wasn't hurt by that, or at least she didn't think so. They had both agreed five months ago to just one night.

Not a lifetime.

There was a knock on the door. They both turned their heads to see a doctor in the doorway.

"Is this the right room?" she asked, brightly.

"Are you, Dr. Perez?" Agustin asked.

"Yes," she replied. "I understand that someone fainted in the operating room?"

Sharon blushed. "Me."

"You're twenty weeks?" Dr. Perez, asked setting down her bag and taking off her coat as Agustin shut the door to the exam room so they could have some privacy.

"Yes," Sharon said. "I didn't know I was pregnant."

Dr. Perez cocked an eyebrow. "A nurse not knowing she was pregnant?"

"Stress has…interrupted my normal cycle before," Sharon said.

"Ah. I see," Dr. Perez replied. "That is normal. Especially if it's your first too."

"My grandmother, Theresa Gonsalves, had a fall, breaking her hip. I took a leave of absence from my job as a locum nurse and I've been caring for her. I decided to stay in Ushuaia to be with her and I just didn't notice my pregnancy before now." Sharon felt foolish when she said it out loud, but it was the truth.

"Theresa Gonsalves is your grandmother? She's a respected midwife." Dr. Perez smiled.

"Yes," Sharon replied.

"She delivered me," Agustin quipped.

"And me," Dr. Perez stated, grinning. "I hope she's doing better."

"She is. I take care of her and I have workers sit with her while I work," Sharon said.

"And who is taking care of you?" Dr. Perez asked sternly. "The father?"

"I am…the father," Agustin responded. "I only just found out as well."

Dr. Perez was stunned, but only for a moment.

"Ah, well, how fortunate you're here. Let's take your blood pressure and check your sugars. We'll book an ultrasound, but I have my Doppler here to listen to the heartbeat."

Her ears pricked up at that. "Really?"

Dr. Perez smiled. "Yes, well, you would've heard it via Doppler by now had you been to a checkup. You can sit up and I'll check your blood pressure."

Sharon sat up as Dr. Perez put the cuff around her arm. She took a deep breath as the cuff squeezed her arm.

"Your blood pressure is a little high, but that could be from the fainting spell and the situation you have at home. We'll check your sugars and then I'm going to send you out to get a bunch of blood tests."

"Okay," Sharon said. There was no point in arguing. Not that she would.

She was pregnant and knew the tests needed to be done. Her blood sugars were measured through a finger prick.

"Blood looks good," Dr. Perez said, writing down the info. "You were complaining of nausea?"

"Yes."

"She shouldn't still have morning sickness, should she?" Agustin asked.

Dr. Perez looked up at them. "She could. She may also have hyperemesis gravidarum, but we'll know for sure after some tests. I think Sharon was a bit dehydrated and that's why she fainted. You need to take breaks, Sharon."

Agustin gave her a knowing look and Sharon tried not to chuckle.

"Still, I want you to have a fasting glucose test," Dr. Perez said.

"Okay, when?" Sharon asked.

"As soon you can arrange it." Dr. Perez pulled out her Doppler. "If you lift your shirt we can see if we can find the heartbeat."

Sharon lay back. Agustin was close by, hovering and looking worried.

"Cold gel," Dr. Perez warned, squirting it on Sharon's belly. Sharon winced, because she forgot how cold that ultrasound gel was. She hoped the heartbeat was strong and she was blaming herself a bit for not knowing she was pregnant sooner.

How could she be so obtuse?

Then she heard static, then there it was: something she heard whenever she worked on a job in obstetrics. The rapid beat of a heart, and it wasn't hers. Her eyes filled with tears at the sound making the reality of this pregnancy all the more real to her in this moment.

She was going to have a baby. She was pregnant.

"Strong heartbeat!" Dr. Perez exclaimed.

Agustin grinned from ear to ear. He murmured, "I can't believe it."

"Believe it." Sharon laughed nervously.

Dr. Perez wiped off Sharon's belly and then her Doppler.

"I will see you tomorrow at nine in the morning, Sharon. I'll have the lab requisitions and we'll book a proper dating ultrasound." Dr. Perez gathered up her equipment.

"We'll be there," Agustin announced.

"If I can get someone to sit with abuela," Sharon argued. "Maria has tomorrow morning off."

"Sandrine will sit with your abuela," Agustin said.

"You're sure?" Sharon asked.

Agustin nodded. "She will be glad to."

Sharon didn't say anything else, but she was annoyed he was overstepping his bounds and the boundaries she had set up, making decisions without consulting her.

"Good," Dr. Perez said. "See you both tomorrow."

"I'll walk you out," Agustin said, leading Dr. Perez out of the exam room.

Sharon sat up, feeling frustrated. Sandrine had sat with her abuela before, or so Maria had told her. Still, he'd just decided and Sharon didn't like that one bit.

She didn't want Agustin interfering in her life, especially if he was just planning on leaving her and their child anyway.

Sharon could take care of herself. She always had. She was the one she could rely on.

Only her.

CHAPTER SIX

AGUSTIN MADE SHARON wait for him at the clinic as he walked back home to retrieve his car. She thankfully didn't argue with him about the importance of prenatal exercise, like she had that morning, especially after her fainting spell. It was for the best she didn't walk home to her abuela's.

He wasn't taking no for an answer and she wasn't fighting.

In fact, he was getting the feeling that she was a bit miffed at him for carrying her out of the operating room. Usually he didn't carry staff out of the operating room, but he'd acted first and hadn't really think about the impact.

He needed to take care of her.

Agustin just wanted to get Sharon back home and settled. When he saw her collapse it had scared him to his very core. He'd tried to get to her in time, but all he'd managed to do was keep her head from smacking the floor.

Dr. Nunez, the anesthesiologist, was the one who knew Dr. Perez the OB/GYN and called her for him. Agustin did have to explain that Sharon was pregnant, but he hadn't told anyone that he was the father.

Although, he was sure that others in the clinic would soon find out, since he'd carried her out of the operating room and stayed for the examination.

Agustin was very relieved that she was okay and that Dr. Perez had set up an appointment to see her tomorrow. When he heard that heartbeat over the Doppler it had completely upended his world. He knew then that nothing would be the same.

It melted his own heart to hear it.

It had scared him to hear that little flutter, knowing that it was his child, but still he treasured that moment. He never got to experience that with Luisa. She wasn't very far along when she died. So to finally hear the heartbeat of a child of his was a bit world-shattering for him.

He had to do better. He had to protect them.

When Dr. Perez had asked her who was taking care of her, he hadn't hesitated in stepping up and taking over. He was part of this pregnancy. Even though Sharon didn't want a relationship, she had made that clear, they were bound together by that little baby.

When he pulled into the driveway, Sandrine was there and she wasn't alone. She had her arms around a young man and Agustin knew exactly what they were doing. His fingers curled into a fist.

Diego. Again.

He knew the boy well and wasn't a fan of his.

His mother had told him all about Diego because it was something his father had grappled with before he died. Sandrine was too young to get so serious over a boy.

Agustin cleared his throat as he came up the path. Sandrine and Diego startled. Agustin just glared as the boy ran down the steps and past him, waving at Sandrine as he left.

"You scared him off," Sandrine complained.

"He's not supposed to be here," Agustin stated.

"He's my boyfriend."

"I don't trust him."

"Why?" Sandrine asked. "You don't know him."

"Father didn't like him either," Agustin said gruffly.

"How would you know that? You never came around when Father was alive."

It stung, but it was true. His father hadn't told him that because they hadn't had a relationship. His father had tried, but Agustin hadn't been interested and now it was too late.

It was no lie he blamed his father for the breakup of his parents. His father had cheated and broken his mother's heart.

It had been hard to forgive his father and easy to ignore he existed when he'd been in Buenos Aires and happy with Luisa.

Even when he came back to Ushuaia, he'd tried to be in his father's life to get to know Sandrine, but he had still been angry at his father.

So Sandrine was right. He was never around.

Agustin crossed his arms. "Father told my mother and my mother filled me in. She loves you, even though she's not your mother, and she wanted to let me know what was happening."

Sandrine rolled her eyes and he knew that she was thinking something like *as if you cared*, but she didn't say the words. He did care, but it was hard to reach and establish a relationship with a younger sibling who he'd only seen a couple of times when he was a young man.

It had nothing to do with Sandrine's birth and everything to do with their father destroying his mother's heart by leaving her for Sandrine's mother. It wasn't Sandrine's fault. It was just hard to reach out.

"Why are you here without your dry cleaning?" Sandrine asked.

"I came to get my car. I walked to work with Sharon this morning and now I have to go pick up Sharon."

"Is Sharon okay?" Sandrine asked, genuinely concerned.

"She is. You know she's pregnant?"

Sandrine nodded. "Yeah, but I don't think she did. Her abuela knew though. Theresa is smart and told me."

Agustin smiled. "She is. Well, I'm the father."

Sandrine looked confused, her eyes wide. "What?"

"Five months ago Sharon and I met in Barcelona and…" Agustin could feel the heat rising up his neck and he ran his fingers through his hair. "Needless to say, I'm the father. The baby is mine."

Sandrine smiled, her eyes twinkling. "I'm going to be an aunt! That's so awesome."

Agustin was stunned. "You're excited?"

"Of course. I love kids." Sandrine clapped her hands. "This is so great!"

Agustin shook his head, but secretly he

was happy that Sandrine was happy about this whole thing. "I'm going to go pick her up and bring her home. Can you sit with Theresa tomorrow so I can take Sharon to a prenatal appointment?"

Sandrine nodded. "Of course! Can I go over to Theresa's house now for a visit and tell her?"

"She doesn't know I'm the father yet. Maybe we should let Sharon tell her, but you can definitely go over there and sit with her and Maria."

Sandrine nodded and clapped her hands as she ran next door. He hadn't seen his sister this happy in…well, ever.

At least with Sandrine at Theresa's she wouldn't be with Diego.

Agustin went inside and grabbed his keys, then headed to his car to drive back to the clinic to get Sharon. Sharon was sitting outside and looked miserable. He hoped that she wasn't still feeling that morning sickness.

He parked the car and then ran to the passenger side and opened the door for her. "Are you okay?"

"I'm fine," she said quietly as she climbed in.

Agustin got back into the driver's seat and started the ignition. Sharon wasn't saying anything, she was just staring out the window, and he had the distinct feeling that she was mad at him.

"Sharon?"

"You're going to ask if I'm mad at you?" she asked.

"Yes."

"Not mad. Annoyed, but not mad." Yet she still wouldn't look at him.

"You can't even look me in the eye."

She turned her head slowly. "That better?"

"What has got you annoyed?"

"You spoke for me. Made the appointment, arranged for care and didn't ask me anything. What if I don't like Dr. Perez?"

"You don't like Dr. Perez?" he asked.

Sharon sighed. "I never said that. She seems great, but the point was you spoke for me. I don't go for that macho attitude or whatever. I am in charge of my life and I make the decisions regarding my body, my baby and my abuela. Got it?"

"Understood. I'm sorry, I overstepped and got a little bit excited. Would you like me to call and cancel?" he offered.

"No. I'll go if Sandrine can sit with Abuela."

"She can. And I told her you're pregnant with my child. She knew you were pregnant, but didn't know I was the father."

Sharon groaned. "Great. Everyone is Ushuaia is going to know my business."

"Because I told my sister?"

"No, my abuela," she chuckled. "Oh, and carrying me out of the operating room."

"Sharon, you're starting to show, and if I hang around you too much people are going to put two and two together."

Sharon laughed softly, breaking the tension that had been in the car since he picked her up. "I suppose you're right. This time."

He grinned. "Thank you for conceding to me, this time."

They shared a smile.

"I am glad you were there when I fainted. I'm so mortified I fainted in the operating room." She shook her head.

"Don't be embarrassed. I'm glad I was there too."

They didn't say much after that and he was relieved that she was no longer annoyed with him. He remembered his late wife getting upset with him too.

Why are you always working? Luisa had said, sobbing.

To build a life for us. I need to work. I'm the low man at the hospital, he'd explained.

Work is more important than me.

He'd pulled Luisa close. *No, never.*

The thing was, she hadn't been totally wrong about that. He had worked a lot and he'd missed a lot. It was why she'd gotten into that car by herself. If he had been with her... Well, there was nothing he could've done to stop the accident.

There was no changing the past.

When they got to Sharon's house Sandrine flung open the door and was all smiles as Sharon walked up the path.

"I didn't say anything to your abuela about my brother being the father, but I am so excited about becoming an aunt," Sandrine said excitedly. She threw her arms around Sharon and hugged her, which surprised him and caught Sharon off guard as well.

Sharon chuckled softly and patted Sandrine's back, still in a bit of shock. "Well, I am very glad to hear it and I want to thank you for giving up your time tomorrow to sit with my grandmother while I go to my appointment."

"Any time I can help out Maria or you, just ask. I really like your grandmother." Sandrine was beaming and her hazel eyes were twinkling. Agustin couldn't ever recall seeing Sandrine this happy since his arrival back in Argentina, and from what his mother had told him it seemed she wasn't exactly a happy child, except when she'd been around his father.

They all walked inside and Sharon's abuela was sitting up at the kitchen table with a puzzle. Sandrine sat back down at the table, working on the puzzle with the elderly lady.

"*Querida*, you're home!" Abuela cocked her head to one side. "You have something to tell me."

Sharon smiled nervously and hung up her coat. "I do. You remember Dr. Agustin Varela?"

"Agustin? Of course, I delivered him. I may have hit my head but I can still remember," her abuela said, pointing to her temple. "I'm only eighty. I'm not dead yet."

Agustin chuckled softly to himself and Sharon rolled her eyes.

"Abuela, Agustin is the father of my baby. We met in Barcelona, before I moved here. I was at a conference and…well, I didn't know he was from Ushuaia and he didn't know I was either…"

Sharon's abuela grinned. "Well, that's excellent news. I don't know what kind of medical conference includes hanky-panky, but I understand why it happened."

Sharon's face flushed red and Agustin couldn't help but laugh.

"Abuela, really," Sharon warned.

Abuela just waved her hand in her direction, dismissing her as she turned to Sandrine. "How do you feel about being an aunt?"

"I'm thrilled," Sandrine exclaimed. "We're going to be family. A real family, finally!"

Agustin felt a twinge of guilt at what Sandrine said about family. Wasn't he family enough for his half sister? Only, he knew the answer. He had never been around for her before because of his strained relationship with his father.

He felt bad that Sandrine was obviously missing something.

"Now you can call me Abuela for real," Theresa stated.

Sandrine gave the old woman a side hug and Sharon just crossed her arms and shook her head.

"You need to rest," Agustin whispered.

"Yes," Sharon agreed.

"I'm going to pick up my dry cleaning and I will get some dinner."

He wanted to put some distance between all this. He wasn't sure what he was feeling right now. He just knew he had to clear his head.

Sharon worried her bottom lip. "You don't have to do that…"

"I want to and I'm not taking no for an answer. I'll be back in a while."

Sharon sighed, but nodded.

He left the house to head back to his hotel.

It was a very cozy scene. Sandrine was happy and bubbly. Sharon's abuela was thrilled, although Sharon still looked a bit out of sorts. Not that he could blame her—he was still feeling a bit out of sorts about the whole thing too. It was like they were forming this little family, and he liked that a lot, but then Sharon didn't want a relationship with him and he couldn't have a relationship with her.

The idea of family was scary. There was no certainty of a happily-ever-after. All he had to do was look at his parents or think about what happened to him and the pain he felt when Luisa died. He had fallen for that ideal of happiness and love once before.

The fairy tale hadn't ended well for him.

Sharon had been so angry at Agustin for making decisions without consulting her, but she was glad she was able to talk to him about it. She was having misgivings about how involved he was trying to be in her life. She wasn't used to that.

Their baby's life, fine, but now he was picking up dinner for them? Sandrine and her abuela looked extremely happy together and Sharon was glad for that, but what was going to happen to them when Agustin decided he'd had enough and found someone to create a real family with? Someone who wanted that happily-ever-after?

It was all too much.

Don't stress yourself out.

Sharon was worried that her blood pressure reading was high, higher than usual for her, and she had been a big ball of stress since she came back to Argentina. Not only navigating all the old memories of her past, but also trying to help her grandmother heal.

"Your mail is on the table there," Sandrine said. "There's a large pile of it. I think Maria forgot to get it the other day."

"Thanks, Sandrine," Sharon said. She made her way to the table and picked up the stack of letters and cards and then saw something that made her blood run cold. A statement from the bank that looked ominous and was addressed to her abuela.

Sharon took the letter into the small sitting room to read it over. Her stomach knotted as she read about back taxes on a property her abuela owned in Buenos Aires and overdue legal fees. Sharon glanced over her shoulder at her abuela sitting there. It was a lot of money, money that Sharon didn't have ready.

Sandrine left the room and Sharon went to her grandmother, sitting next to her.

"Abuela, you own property in Buenos Aires?" She handed her grandmother the letter.

"No. I don't think so." Abuela stared at the letter. "I don't understand. I sold this five years ago."

"You did?" Sharon asked, confused.

"*Sí.* Five years ago. My accountant back then took care of it. Arranged Realtors and everything." Her abuela rubbed her head. "At least, I think so. I remember paying taxes on it before."

Sharon took back the letter. "Well, try not to worry. We'll figure it out."

Abuela nodded. "I'm sorry to burden you with it."

"I might have to get a power of attorney."

Abuela frowned. "Okay, but talk to your aunt too. Maybe she knows."

"I will."

She was going to have to talk to her aunt and see if there was any kind of paperwork and try to work this out. She knew her abuela would sign over a power of attorney so Sharon could talk to the bank in Buenos Aires.

She had some time to get this figured out, but the threat was clear and it was exactly what she didn't need right at this moment. Sharon took the letter and slipped it into her purse.

Sharon would take care of it, just like she'd taken care of a lot of things throughout her life since her mother died and her father abandoned her. She could rely on herself. She didn't need to rely on anyone else.

It was better this way.

She leaned her head back against the couch cushions and could feel the baby moving inside her. It was the first time she'd really ever paid attention to it and she smiled as she felt it whiz under her skin. She placed a hand on her slightly rounded belly. The baby moved under her fingers, but she wasn't sure if she could feel it through her belly or if it was just because she could feel the baby moving within her. Either way, it made her smile even more.

"I will try," she whispered to the baby. "You won't want for anything and you won't be alone."

The baby nudged her and she laughed, fighting back the tears that were threatening to spill. It annoyed her how much her emotions were going up and down today. It was not like her at all and she really did hate this loss of control, especially when it came to Agustin.

There was a knock and the door opened as Agustin came back in with takeaway bags. A swirl of snow followed him in.

"It's really snowing out there," he panted.

Sandrine helped him with the bags and brought them into the kitchen. Their gazes locked across the room.

"Are you okay?" he asked, his voice full of concern, which made her heart melt just a bit. She couldn't let herself fall for him.

He'd leave her. He'd made it clear he didn't want a relationship, just as she had, and she couldn't risk her heart.

"Fine," she replied, plastering a fake smile on her face. "Thanks for bringing dinner."

He nodded and slipped off his shoes and took off his coat.

She sighed and stood up. She had to keep reminding herself this little bloom of happiness, in this moment, with Agustin, his sister, her abuela and her was temporary. Happiness never lasted forever and she had to be ready when the bubble burst.

CHAPTER SEVEN

SHARON WAS LOOKING out at the window absently, staring at the snow when she saw Sandrine coming down the street.

She was with Diego.

A local boy.

Someone Agustin seemed to detest. It was a good thing Agustin wasn't here.

Actually, she hadn't seen him in a couple of weeks. It had been that long since she'd collapsed in the operating room and her first checkup with Dr. Perez.

Sandrine kissed her boyfriend goodbye outside and then came bounding up the steps into her abuela's home.

The young girl had taken it upon herself to come over and visit them after school, which Sharon didn't mind in the least.

It broke her heart to think of Sandrine lonely.

Sharon keenly remembered how it had been for her as a young child.

Abandoned.

Her aunt liked to think she'd forgotten, but Sharon hadn't. Although Sandrine hadn't been abandoned the way that she had, their situations were still similar. It was like looking at a younger version of herself.

A parallel.

The difference between Sandrine and her: Sandrine was older than she had been.

Sharon wasn't sure that made a difference. Maybe Sandrine hadn't been so blindsided when her mother had left her, because she mentioned often that her mother was never around.

No matter how it had happened, it was wrong.

It was heartbreaking.

Something she knew firsthand.

"*Hola*, Sharon," Sandrine said brightly. "Is Abuela asleep?"

"She is," Sharon said. "How was school?"

"Good. We've been talking about careers." Sandrine set her bag down and slipped off her shoes to come sit in the living room.

"Any thoughts?" Sharon asked, interested.

"Gus wants me to be a surgeon," Sandrine

responded, using the name Sharon had first known Agustin by.

"How do you feel about that?"

"It's a lot of schooling. Diego wants to be a mechanic and stay here."

Now it made sense why Agustin was wary of Diego's influence. Medical school was far away and trade school was here in Ushuaia.

"Is that why your brother dislikes Diego, because he might be swaying you?" Sharon asked.

Sandrine blushed. "Maybe."

"Look…"

"You're not going to hate on him now too, are you?" Sandrine asked, hurt.

"No. I don't know him. He seems nice."

Sandrine nodded. "He is. You'll see when you get to know him properly."

The problem was Sharon wasn't sure that was possible. With the back taxes her abuela owed on a property she'd thought was sold, Sharon was considering the real possibility of selling the house. It was clear the accountant had absconded with the money and the property was never put up for sale. Her abuela's memories were hazy and Sharon was struggling to find out information.

She would have to go to Buenos Aires, as the property was there. Each province had their own set of rules, so she couldn't figure this out in Ushuaia.

The legal fees were high and if she sold this home as well as the property in Buenos Aires she could discharge the back taxes and pay the legal fees. The only way to do both was to sell this home though. Once that was all done, then she'd have to find a small apartment or affordable small home for her, her abuela and her baby to live.

Which might mean they'd be on the other side of town.

It worried her how she was going to break the news to her abuela as well.

Her grandmother seemed to be getting attached to the idea that Agustin and Sandrine were going to be part of their lives going forward.

Which was not a certainty.

Her abuela was too trusting, too caring, which was why everyone in the community loved her so much and probably why she'd been taken advantage of five years ago.

Sharon felt her stomach dip, a wave of nausea hitting her as she thought of the mess her life had become since Barcelona. How complicated and involved with others it had become.

She'd talked to her aunt in New York and her aunt had referred her to a lawyer so she could get a power of attorney to deal with the back taxes, but it was a mess and stressful.

Between her work, caring for her abuela and her pregnancy, it was hard to conduct it all over the phone and email in Ushuaia.

"Sharon, are you okay?" Sandrine asked.

"No." And she didn't feel okay at all. Her head was pounding and she felt so nauseous. It was worrying. She got up and checked her blood pressure. It was high.

A bunch of scenarios ran through her head, but her head began to ache. She knew one thing: she had to get checked out. "Can you call an ambulance for me, Sandrine?"

"Sí." Sandrine made a call and Sharon sat on the floor. The room was spinning. Sandrine was talking to other people and she felt a blast of cold air as the front door was opened.

"What's wrong?" Agustin asked, his voice panicked.

"The ambulance is on its way," Sandrine said, but it sounded like she was far away.

"Keep Theresa calm." Agustin dropped to her side. *"Querida?"*

Sharon could hear her abuela panicking in the background and Sandrine comforting her.

"I feel dizzy again." And that was all she could manage to say before everything faded to black.

* * *

Agustin was beside himself as he paced outside Sharon's hospital room door. He had kept away for a couple of weeks and immersed himself in work, because he thought it was for the best to put some distance between them.

Sharon also seemed off since the operating room incident.

He didn't want to scare her away by being too involved in her life, but it was killing him to keep away.

Sharon threw up some emotional wall after that night and he'd gotten the hint to back off. So he'd gone back to the thing he knew well, where he didn't have to think about emotions or anything.

Work.

Then Sandrine had texted him.

Sharon was ill and an ambulance had been called.

It was like a nightmare. He couldn't even ride in the ambulance with her because he wasn't related to her.

So, all he could do was pace.

Dr. Perez came out of the room.

"Well?" Agustin asked.

"Her blood pressure was a bit high, but it's under control. She's still having morning sickness and she's dehydrated. She's staying here until the bolus of fluids is done and then she needs to go home and rest for a couple of days."

Agustin was relieved. "Can I see her?"

"For a little bit. I'd like her to rest until I'm happy with her electrolytes. I'll let you know when I'm discharging her."

"*Gracias*, Dr. Perez."

Agustin entered the room and Sharon was scowling at the ceiling.

"How are you now?" Agustin asked.

"Annoyed," she stated. "Dr. Perez wants me to rest."

"And you should." He sat down in the chair.

"I like to work," she stated.

"I understand," he chuckled.

"What's so funny?" she asked indignantly.

"Doctors are not the only ones to make lousy patients."

She smiled, the annoyance melting away. "I suppose not. I like control. It feels like I have none of that in my life right now."

"I understand."

"Sandrine said they were talking about careers at school. She said you wanted her to be a surgeon."

"*Sí*. I do," he responded.

"Why?" she asked.

He groaned inwardly. It seemed to personal.

He wanted Sandrine to be independent and not like her mother.

"She's smart," he said.

"Agreed."

He ran his hand through his hair. "She's capable and it would give her freedom."

"Is that why you wanted to be a doctor?" she asked.

"These are a lot of questions," he groused.

Sharon shrugged. "What else have I got to do."

"Fine. Yes, partly. I just loved helping people, saving lives…" He trailed off as he thought of Luisa and how he couldn't save her.

Sometimes medicine failed.

"So why did you become a nurse?" he asked, changing the subject to her.

"Same. I wanted independence and a nurse was…was kind to me when I was young. I wanted to help others."

"Very noble." He smiled and took her hand without thinking. It was so small in his.

So fragile.

Just like the little life growing inside her.

He let go of her hand and stood up. "You need rest."

She nodded. "Okay. My abuela?"

"Sandrine is holding down the fort. I'll go

check on them too. I'll come back to pick you up when you're discharged."

"Thank you," she said.

He nodded and left the room. He was getting too attached to Sharon.

It was clear this pregnancy was hard on her.

He was terrified something was going to happen to the baby, to her.

He wasn't sure his heart could handle it if something did.

Sharon had been off work for a week since her episode, which required her to get intravenous treatment for dehydration.

Finally she was given some shifts.

It had been worrying her she hadn't been working. She needed to work as much as possible before the baby came.

She wasn't even annoyed she got light duties at the clinic, which was dealing with a lot of patients who were there for Botox or consults.

She was working and that was all that mattered.

Agustin was keeping his distance too. Which was fine on one hand, but on the other, she missed him.

Something had changed in her hospital room and she wasn't sure what it was.

"You ready for the ultrasound?" Agustin asked, coming into the office where she had been working on her final preoperative assessment reports.

"What?" she asked, shaking her head of all the thoughts that were going around and around inside her.

"It's four o'clock. Our ultrasound is scheduled in fifteen minutes. Are you ready?"

"Right." She shook her head again and closed the file she was working on. "Sorry, I just zoned out there for a moment."

"You're not dizzy, are you?" he asked, worry in his voice.

"No. And no nausea either. Just preoccupied."

Which was true.

She was.

There was a lot going on.

"If you're sure," he hedged.

"I'm fine. Let's go," she responded.

She wasn't too pleased with this babying. She knew how to take care of herself.

Agustin had her coat in his hand. It was just a quick walk to the building next door. It was the same building Dr. Perez worked out of and where she had her blood work done. They walked outside and it was snowing and hazy out.

It had been a stormy June so far.

She slipped a bit on an icy patch and Agustin reached out and steadied her. His hand on her back, even through her thick winter coat, was warming. She could feel her body responding to his simple touch.

"Thank you," she whispered.

"No need to thank me." Agustin opened the door and they made their way inside. They were taken straightaway to a room and Sharon was made comfortable on exam bed, while Agustin stood next to her.

He was very tense.

Or maybe that was her stress.

"Are you okay?" she asked, lying there with her hands folded on her chest.

"Fine," he replied stiffly.

"I don't think so."

He didn't look at her. "Okay. I'm not."

She wanted to ask him why he wasn't when the ultrasound technician walked into the room.

"*Hola!* My name is Mariposa and I'm your ultrasound technician today." She was readying her equipment. "Sharon, you drank all your water?"

"Yes. I'm ready to burst."

Mariposa laughed gently. "Everyone says

that. Now if you could lift your shirt and slide your pants down, I've got some towels here."

Sharon and Mariposa exposed her rounder pregnant belly.

"You're about twenty-two weeks?" Mariposa asked.

"Twenty-three," Agustin responded.

"Yes," Sharon said. "Just twenty-three."

"Oh, then we may be able to tell the gender. Would you like to know the gender?" Mariposa asked.

Sharon glanced over at Agustin. "Well, would we?"

"I would like to know," he said.

Sharon smiled. "So would I."

"Great! Just going to put some gel on your belly and we'll get started." Mariposa squeezed the ultrasound gel on her belly and Sharon watched the monitor, waiting for that first glimpse of the little surprise that she had never been expecting.

It only took a few moments for the blurry black-and-white image to show a small staticky-looking baby on the screen. Sharon's heart caught in her throat—she never really had understand that expression until this moment, but now, looking at the baby she never thought she'd ever have, she felt it.

Just like that night after she collapsed and felt the baby under her fingers.

It was magical.

"Looks very healthy," Mariposa remarked, taking pictures and measurements.

Sharon glanced over at Agustin, but he wasn't saying anything. His face was unreadable, but he reached down and took her hand and squeezed it, his gaze fixed on the screen. She wasn't sure what he was feeling in that moment seeing their child, but she knew what she was feeling and that was love.

Love for that little life.

Her child.

She would never let anyone hurt her child. Her child would never face the trauma she had. Her child would always know love and never loneliness. She made that vow silently to herself.

"Would you like to know the gender now?" Mariposa asked, interrupting her thoughts.

"*Sí*," Sharon whispered, holding her breath.

"It's a girl. Congratulations," Mariposa said brightly.

A tear slid from Sharon's cheek and Agustin knelt down beside her and touched her face, wiping the tear away with the pad of his thumb. They locked gazes and her heart felt like it was going to burst, sharing this special moment with him. It meant so much to her, but she had to remember to guard her heart and not melt for him, but here she was in this moment doing just that.

"I'll get you both a picture," Mariposa said brightly. She handed Sharon another towel to clean up and then she left the room.

Agustin helped her sit up as she wiped the gel off her belly.

"How do you feel?" he asked, finding his voice.

"Great. I am happy, but I would be happy whatever it was as long as it's healthy."

Agustin nodded. "Same, but I can't help, in this moment, feeling just a little bit happy at the thought of a daughter. Especially if she looks like you."

The tender comment caught her off guard and she could feel the blush creeping up her neck. "Thank you."

"Shall we go out to dinner and celebrate? Sandrine is with your grandmother tonight."

"Did you preplan dinner?" Sharon asked.

"I did." He grinned and winked. "Come on, I know the perfect little place just outside of town. It's a hotel, but serves a great little dinner overlooking the Beagle Channel."

Sharon cocked an eyebrow. "You want to drive down to the channel in this weather?"

"It's clearing up. We'll be fine and it's early. Come." He held out his hand and even though she thought the idea of going to have dinner out of town seemed silly, it was Friday and the clinic was closed tomorrow and she wasn't on duty.

It might be nice and relaxing to have dinner down by the water. There wouldn't be as many tourists as that road out of town that headed to the national park of Lapataia and in June it wasn't the busiest of roads.

It would be peaceful.

Still, the thought of being alone with him unnerved her. She was trying to distance herself from him and if she went with him, she was hardly doing that. Instead of listening to her rational side though, she took his hand as he helped her stand up and get her coat on.

"I'm not really dressed for a fancy place," she remarked.

"It's not that fancy. You're fine. It's just a gorgeous spot." He put his hand on the small of her back and they walked back to the clinic parking lot and he opened the door to his car. She settled into the passenger seat.

The snow had stopped and the sun was going down.

It was one of her favorite times of the day in the winter months. The sky had warm orange tones as the sun set below the western edge, over the mountains that separated Chile and Argentina, but there were various grays and blacks in the sky, signaling a storm and the cold of the winter months.

A time of darkness.

It was the time of year that always made her feel cozy. She just wasn't quite used to having this feeling in June, which for her had always been the mark of summer.

"I have forgotten what a June winter feels like. I'm going to have to get used to the idea of a warm Christmas," she said brightly.

"I'm used to it. It's the cold I struggle with. Always have."

"Your mother is in Buenos Aires?"

"Yes. She's originally from there, so when her marriage to my father ended...not by her choice, she went back home, and that's where I went to medical school. I was in university when they split up. I was at school in Buenos Aires and I stayed there for a long time. I only came back to Ushuaia about five years ago."

"I'm sorry about your parents."

"What about your parents?" he asked.

Sharon swallowed the lump in her throat. She knew this conversation would come eventually, but it was one she didn't want to have.

Burying the pain of her childhood was easier than talking about it constantly. It helped her to move on and create a life for herself.

"My mother died when I was nine, and about six months after that my father walked out of our home in New York City and never came back. Thankfully, my maternal aunt Elisa lived in White Plains, just up the Hudson River with her husband, and she was called."

"Oh, my God…how long were you left on your own?" he asked, shocked.

"A week," she whispered, as the memories of that horrible time came flooding back to her. Her fear of the policemen and not understanding what was wrong. The concerned neighbors. She had lived on cereal and whatever she could reach for that week.

Her aunt had been beside herself, trying not to cry as she spoke to the policeman. Sharon had just clung to her dolly, not sure of what was happening.

"I'm sorry that happened to you, *querida*," he whispered.

He'd called her that before. She never paid it any mind until now.

After sharing that bit about herself, the word meant something else now.

She wasn't his dearest.

"What?"

"Querida," he said again. "Dearest. I think

it's fitting. You are the mother of my child, or rather my daughter."

She liked when he said it and she shouldn't.

It's what her abuela and her aunt had called her. Everyone in her family, and it just seemed right. She really hoped that he couldn't see the warmth spreading in her cheeks. Still, she was annoyed she was letting him affect her like this.

"Did they ever find your father?" Agustin asked quietly.

"No. I don't know what happened to him. My aunt did obtain guardianship, so he sent in something, but there was no return address. I have no idea what happened to him and I really don't care. You don't know where Sandrine's mother is, do you?"

Agustin sighed. "No. I don't. She left that poor girl all alone, but Sandrine was older and she's told me that she was used to being left. It was just her and our father. She would care for him. I had no concept of how sick he was."

"You didn't come to see him?"

"I never forgave him for what he did to my mother, but my mother is kind. She did forgive Father, probably when she remarried. She was the one that told me Sandrine had been abandoned and the house in Ushuaia was mine.

Thankfully, I was there and not still living in Buenos Aires."

It grew darker as they headed west and away from the lights of Ushuaia. It was then that she saw blinking lights in the distance.

"What's that?" Sharon asked.

Agustin slowed the car and leaned over the wheel. "It looks like a car in the ditch."

"We better pull over and check."

Agustin nodded and slowed down more, pulling in behind the car, which was slightly in the ditch, but not completely. As they pulled to a stop a man in his twenties waved at them frantically.

Agustin rolled down his window. "What's wrong?"

The man looked confused, like he didn't understand. "*No hablo Español*. Not very well, that is," the man mumbled.

"American?" Sharon asked, switching to English.

"Yes. Are you American?" the man asked.

"I am. What's wrong?" Sharon asked.

"My wife, we were hiking by Lapataia. We decided to head back to the hotel, but our car hit some ice and we slid off the road. We were okay, but they said it was going to be over an hour to get a tow, and she's in labor and I can't get another cell signal to call an ambulance. Do you have a working cell phone?"

"What's wrong?" Agustin asked, confused.

"His wife is in labor and their cell phone is dead." Sharon turned back to the man. "He's a doctor and I'm a nurse. We'll call an ambulance and then we'll come and check on your wife."

"Oh, thank God," the man said. "I'm Kevin, by the way. My wife is Dana."

Sharon smiled. "I'm Sharon and this is Agustin. Well, Kevin, lead me to your wife and Agustin here will call the ambulance."

Kevin nodded and jogged off, to where she saw his wife had gotten out of the car and was panting, hunched over and leaning on the hood.

Assessing her, Sharon said, "Call an ambulance. I think she can't wait, judging by the pain she's in."

Agustin nodded. "Be careful yourself."

"I will."

Agustin pulled out his phone and Sharon carefully got out of the car. She made her way over to the couple and that was when she noticed the child in the back sleeping. It was a minivan and she knew from stories in the

States that they weren't always the most reliable vehicles when it came to icy roads.

"You have another child? Are they okay?" Sharon asked.

Kevin nodded. "Oh, yeah, they're sleeping. Our son sleeps through anything."

Kevin's wife, Dana, snorted in pain, as if agreeing with him.

"Dana, this is Sharon and she's a nurse."

Dana's blue eyes were glazed over in pain. "Oh, thank goodness."

"Let's get you in the back of your van. Do you have blankets?" Sharon asked.

Kevin nodded. "Yeah, we have our whole life in that van. We drove down from Alaska."

Sharon's eyes widened. "Wow. So, no prenatal care?"

"I gave birth to Dylan at home," Dana panted. "I'm fine."

Sharon nodded. "Okay, well, let's check on you."

Kevin and Sharon managed to get Dana into the back of the van. There was a bed set up and she was so thankful that there was a place to get Dana comfortable.

"Did your water break?" Sharon asked, climbing into the back of the van as she got Dana settled.

"Yes," Dana said breathlessly through contractions.

Kevin helped his wife remove her trousers and covered her with a sheet. Agustin came over then with a first aid kit.

"Thought you might need this, or rather *we* might need this." He smiled. "The ambulance is on its way."

"What's he saying?" Kevin asked.

"Agustin said the ambulance is on its way," Sharon said. "Agustin, can you help me?"

Agustin nodded. He peeled off his jacket and opened the first aid kit. They quickly sanitized their hands and put on disposable gloves that were supplied. It wasn't much, but it was something.

"I'm going to check you now," Sharon said to Dana.

Dana nodded. Kevin held her hand. Agustin shone a light for Sharon to see. She felt and could feel the baby's head and it was right there.

"Oh," Sharon exclaimed. "Your baby is getting ready to crown, so I think it's okay to start pushing."

"Really?" Dana asked.

Sharon quickly translated for Agustin, who smiled that charming smile that would put anyone at ease. His sleeves had been rolled up and he handed the flashlight to Kevin as he squatted and got ready to catch the baby.

"Have you delivered a baby before?" Sharon asked Agustin.

"I have. I don't think you can kneel down here in your condition," Agustin remarked.

She didn't even bother arguing with him—he was right. There was no way that she could get down there in such a confined space, in these conditions.

"You're right," she murmured.

"Dana," Agustin said.

"Yes?" she asked.

"Push...next...contraction," Agustin managed in English. "Baby is here."

Dana nodded and Sharon urged her to push as the contraction tightened across Dana's belly. Dana cried and Agustin encouraged her in Spanish. It didn't matter, it was translating well as the little baby was in a hurry and wasn't waiting for any ambulance to make its way from Ushuaia to here.

It only took a couple of pushes. The baby's shoulders were free and the rest of the little boy slipped out and into Agustin's arms.

The baby didn't cry.

"I need a blanket," Agustin said, keeping

his voice calm, but she could hear the stress, the serious undertone.

This baby might die.

"Why isn't the baby crying?" Dana asked.

Sharon scrambled down next to Agustin, handing him clean blankets as he flipped the baby and massaged his back, trying to keep him in the warmth of the back of the van. He slapped the baby on the back as Sharon knelt down, rubbing the baby's face and body, trying to coax a cry.

"He's not breathing," Agustin whispered. He flipped the baby back over and set him down, tilting the little head back and checking the baby's airway. He began giving rescue breaths and Sharon could see the baby's little chest rising. Agustin then started compressions with his fingers.

He only had to do it once and the baby let out a gasp and screamed.

Sharon hadn't realized that she was holding her breath. She held out the blanket as Agustin grinned and clamped and cut the cord, using what limited supplies were available, before placing the baby into the blanket.

"Bueno," Agustin proclaimed, giving a thumbs-up to the worried parents.

"You have a boy," Sharon proclaimed, placing the little boy in Dana's arms.

Dana was crying and held her boy, but then her face contorted and Sharon had a sinking feeling that it wasn't the placenta.

"She's contracting again," Sharon told Agustin.

"Again?" Agustin asked, checking. "There's another head."

"She didn't know. She didn't have prenatal care," Sharon explained.

Agustin said nothing. Just frowned as he went to work.

Kevin took his son and a little girl entered the world just as quickly, but the moment she was free of her mother in Agustin's arms she screamed lustily.

Agustin chuckled and looked at Sharon tenderly.

Sharon was fighting back tears, watching Agustin with those little babies that were in such a hurry to be born on the side of the road in Tierra del Fuego. They were so small in his strong arms and she couldn't help but think of their own little girl as he handed the baby over to her mother.

Sharon just smiled at him in awe and they heard the wail of the ambulance coming up the road. Kevin, Dana and the now awake little Dylan were all cuddled in the back of the van, a happy family.

Sharon envied them.

She wished she had what they had. Maybe not a roadside birth, but Agustin's love, their children.

A family.

Agustin was finally able to make it to the place he wanted to take Sharon for dinner, but they were a little worse for wear after helping deliver a baby in the tight confines of the car, so he ordered takeout and then drove down to a secluded spot that overlooked the channel.

It was not what he'd envisioned, but he was glad they'd both been there to help that family.

When that little baby was born and wasn't breathing, he'd had a flashback to the moment he lost Luisa.

The same terror that gripped him when Sharon collapsed twice.

Thankfully, the baby had pulled through, and Sharon had been a huge help in making that happen. She'd been as steady as a rock through it all.

They had been true partners in that moment.

That little American family seemed like a tight-knit group. They were so full of love. He had that kind of love from his mother, but not really from his father.

Although there were blurry memories from his past that were starting to creep back out from where he'd tightly locked them away.

There'd been some happy times.

He wanted that.

He wanted that loving family, that tight-knit group.

It's why he got married all those years ago.

Love and the hope of happiness.

He was a bit more jaded now.

He glanced over at Sharon, whose eyes were twinkling as she ate her dinner out of a cardboard box in his car, and his heart swelled.

There were a lot of emotions running through him at the ultrasound today. When he saw that little fetus on the screen, he was filled with emotions that he hadn't experienced in a long time, but the sense of dread was still there.

He couldn't help it.

All he could think about was losing Luisa. All he could think about was how much she had been looking forward to her ultrasound and seeing their child and he couldn't seem to let go of Luisa's accident. How work had taken priority that night and she'd driven in bad weather alone.

He'd paid the price by losing them. Now he was here in Ushuaia and had this second chance. Agustin didn't feel that he deserved it. He was afraid to feel happy or excited, even though he was.

And when he saw Sharon help that mother, as they delivered those twins, Agustin was just caught up in the love and the happiness and the pride he felt for having Sharon carry his second chance at his dreams.

Only, Sharon wasn't his.

"You're really quiet," Sharon said. "Are you all right?"

"I think I'm still in shock from that set of twins," he said, which he was, but that wasn't what was on his mind tonight. "I wanted you to have a nice dinner, a sit-down dinner, and yet all I can seem to manage is to get you take-away dinners."

Sharon laughed softly in the dim light. "I really do like takeaway dinners. And you have managed to take me out before, you know."

"Oh?"

"The café in Barcelona. I believe we had some lovely sangria and tapas that night."

He grinned. "That's right, we did."

"You forgot about that?" she asked.

"About that night, no, but the café is a dim memory compared to what happened later that evening," he said huskily. It was true—he remembered every exquisite inch of her.

"It's in the forefront of my mind as well," she admitted, and then she reached down to touch her rounded belly. His gaze followed her movement.

"May I?" he asked.

"Touch my belly?" she asked, with a hint of hope in her voice.

"*Sí.* I would like that very much."

"Of course."

Agustin reached over and gently placed a hand on her belly, feeling the fullness of the swell and knowing there was a little life growing in there. His daughter. It was hard to wrap his mind around that idea, that it was his daughter in there and that he was going to be a father in less than twenty weeks.

It was then as he rested his hand on her belly that he felt a little push. Just ever so slight, a nudge against the palm of his hand. His daughter was alive and thriving.

She was real.

He knew logically she was real, but his little girl was reaching out to him and letting him know that she was there. All he felt through his veins in that moment was love, and he wanted to protect her and Sharon.

"Did you feel that?" Sharon asked, her voice excited.

"I did," Agustin responded.

Sharon placed her hand on her belly too and there was another nudge and they both smiled at each other.

"She seems to like your dinner as well," Sharon said teasingly.

"It's good food. I'm glad she has taste." He leaned over the console of the car and touched Sharon's face gently. She closed her eyes. Sharon was so beautiful, that hadn't changed. He pressed a kiss against her forehead. "Thank you, *querida*."

"For what?" she whispered breathlessly.

"For taking good care of our baby."

Sharon smiled and then she leaned over, pressing a kiss against his lips, featherlike, but still like the first time she had kissed him. The memories of that first kiss and then the kisses that had come after that came flooding through him. He cupped her face and deepened that featherlight kiss.

Sharon melted under him, parting her lips. He slipped his tongue into her mouth, tasting her again. He had missed her. Even though she wasn't his, he had missed her and missed this, but then he remembered they had made no promises and he wasn't staying here.

Agustin pulled away. "I'm sorry."

"No, don't be sorry. I encouraged that. It

was just…the baby kicking and that delivery tonight. I got a little caught up in the moment."

His heart was aching as he looked at her, her eyes twinkling in the dark. "We can't let that happen again."

"It won't. I want us to be friends and I want to be able to work together without everything being so awkward."

"I promise. Friends."

Sharon nodded. "Well, we better get back to town. It's getting late and I'm exhausted."

"You're right." Agustin moved back into his seat and fastened his seat belt. "I did have a great time with you today."

Sharon smiled. "Same."

He didn't say anything more as he started the ignition and slowly made his way back to Ushuaia. His blood was still burning, his body still craving her, and a little voice inside him was questioning why he had to leave when everything he wanted was here, but that little voice had forgotten that he'd once had everything, and he couldn't bear the thought of losing that all again.

CHAPTER EIGHT

WHEN THEY GOT back to Ushuaia, Agustin was still struggling with all these emotions and the pain of Luisa dying was suddenly raw and fresh again in his heart. He was torn and didn't know what to do.

This was not what he'd planned when he decided to come back here and deal with his father's estate and his half sister. It was supposed to be easy, but he didn't know why he'd thought that and he could only chalk it up to his optimism. But the moment they walked back into Sharon's abuela's house he didn't have a moment to even think about it, because they were bombarded with questions from his sister and Sharon's abuela about the baby.

It was all a blur as he stood there, and Sandrine was so happy to find out the baby was going to be a little girl.

All he could do was stand there stunned.

What he needed to do was get some space.

"I have a phone call to make," he said quickly. "I'll be back in a bit."

Sharon nodded. "Okay."

He nodded and slipped out the door. He made his way across the yard and unlocked his front door. He took off his jacket, hanging it up, and then made his way over to the bar to pour himself a shot of fernet.

It was then his phone rang, buzzing in the pocket of his trousers.

He pulled it out and it was his mother.

"*Hola*, Mama," he answered. "You're calling me late."

"It's not late," his mother said.

He smiled. "It's late for you."

"Ah, yes, true, but I can't sleep. I thought I would check in on how you and Sandrine are getting along since she left school here."

He chuckled. "You really called because you knew today was the ultrasound."

His mother laughed softly. "I care about Sandrine and you, but yes, I am also curious about how that went."

"It's a girl and she's healthy," Agustin stated.

"A girl?" His mother's voice quivered. "I am so happy."

"I am sure."

"How are you feeling?" his mother asked.

"Fine."

"Come on, I know that you have always had big emotions and you're just like your father and really good at squirreling them away."

Agustin was annoyed that his mother was comparing him to his father. He was nothing like his father, who'd left. His father who had put work above all else.

Aren't you doing the same?

He ignored that little voice in his head, because he didn't have the emotional strength to deal with it right now. There were a lot of emotions going on inside him and he really didn't want to talk about it right now.

His phone buzzed again, but this time it was the postoperative care unit at the clinic. It was a call that he had to take.

"Mama, I need to go, the clinic is calling about one of my patients."

His mother sighed. "Very well. I will call you later in the week. I am very happy about the baby and I can't wait to meet Sharon. Please bring her to Buenos Aires when you can."

"Night, Mama." Agustin ended the call and then answered the call from the clinic. "Agustin speaking."

"Agustin, it's Pilar from the clinic. I'm calling about your patient, Alondra. She's running a very high fever. We tried to get it down, but then the stitches are coming loose and we need your assistance. The patient's family refused to allow anyone else to work on their mother."

"I'll be there." Agustin ended the call.

He grabbed his coat. He opened the front door and found Sharon standing on the front step. She had changed out of her clothes and had braided her hair back. Had he really been on the phone for that long with his mother? He glanced at his watch—he had left Sharon's place over an hour ago.

"Sharon!" he exclaimed.

"You were gone for a while and Sandrine was getting worried. She made a cake." Sharon chuckled.

"Sorry. Phone call and then the clinic called. Alondra is having problems and the family only wants me to deal with it."

"Okay, well, Alondra is a patient I took care of, so can I come and help you?"

Agustin cocked an eyebrow. "Are you going to be okay?"

"I'm fine. I feel great and this is my job. Alondra is my patient too and I want to be there to help."

Agustin nodded. "Very well. Grab your things and we'll head over there."

Sharon scurried over to her abuela's house and was back outside within ten minutes with her purse and a clean pair of scrubs. They got into his car and they headed over to the clinic, neither of them saying much.

When they got there, Sharon headed to the nurses' locker room to change and Agustin went straight into the attending lounge to change into his scrubs. He wasn't sure what they were dealing with, but with symptoms such as pain, high fever and stitches not holding he was worried about some kind of infection.

He wouldn't know until he got in there and examined Alondra.

When he got to Alondra's room Sharon was waiting and had the chart. She was talking to the nurse on duty for the evening.

"What did you notice, Pilar?" Agustin asked the nurse as Sharon handed him the chart.

"Alondra's temperature spiked to one hundred and five and we just couldn't bring it down. I examined the wounds from her tummy tuck and that's when I noticed the stitches coming away. There was some drainage and loss of feeling."

Agustin frowned. "Did you start her on antibiotics?"

Pilar nodded. "I did, but I thought you better take a look. Her husband was quite adamant that you come in and check. He didn't want just a nurse."

Agustin tried not to roll his eyes. He knew Alondra's husband well, or at least knew his reputation well. He'd flown his new wife down from Buenos Aires just to see him. Agustin was good at what he did, but there were days that he missed working in a hospital and being a plastic surgeon that dealt with scalp lacerations or cleft palates.

Working in this private clinic, he didn't often get a chance to work on cases like that and he was beginning to miss it. He was getting tired of the privileged, although sometimes he did get to work on patients that needed construction after cancer, and those patients were always grateful and he was in awe of the battles they'd fought and won.

This patient was privileged and they didn't let him forget it, which was why he was here.

He knocked on the door and entered her private room. "Alondra, I understand you're having some problems."

"That's an understatement," her husband muttered.

Alondra winced. "I don't feel well, Dr. Varela."

Agustin came over to her and checked her vitals. Her pulse was rapid and her heart rate was elevated. He frowned.

"Sharon, I need you to check on the status of her labs. Pilar did a blood draw, and I need a CBC panel to check for signs of infection."

Sharon nodded. "Right away, Agustin."

Sharon slipped out of the room.

"I'm going to examine your incision," Agustin said, gently. "Is that okay, Alondra?"

"Yes." Alondra nodded weakly.

Agustin carefully removed the bandage and saw the signs. Redness, stitches dissolving and the drainage. There were also hard lumps and as he gently palpated she wasn't reacting unless he got near one of the bumps.

It was some kind of bacterial infection, but Agustin had seen this in hospitals. He was pretty sure that it was necrotizing soft tissue. He would have to know which bacteria was causing this and then he could effectively treat it.

"Well?" Max, Alondra's husband, demanded.

"She has an infection. We've ordered blood work and I'm awaiting the results. She's on a dose of penicillin and that will help with the infection, and once I know what strain of bacteria is causing these symptoms then I can tailor the treatment. I will need to do surgical debridement of the wound."

Alondra started to cry softly to herself. "More surgery?"

"The good news is that I think we caught it early," Agustin continued as Max comforted Alondra. "I will keep you posted and I will be here for the rest of the night to check on you. I promise, my nurse Sharon is going to look after you. I understand she was taking care of you before?"

Alondra nodded. "I like her."

"We both do," Max added.

"Good." Agustin left the room and shut the door. Sharon had the lab report and handed it to him. Her face had a grim expression. He read through it and his suspicions were right. It was a bacterial infection and it was one of the ones that often caused necrotizing soft tissue infections.

He sighed and dragged his hand through his hair. At least he knew what it was and how to treat it. "It's Staphylococcus aureus."

Sharon nodded. "You think it's causing her soft tissue in her wound to necrotize?"

"Yes. The drainage from the wound was not healthy. All the signs are there, but we run a sterile operating room, so I'm concerned about how it got in there, unless she already had it and it hadn't appeared yet. Sometimes it can slip blood screens." Agustin tapped his chin, thinking. "She's on penicillin, yes?"

Sharon nodded. "Yes."

"I want her on vancomycin until we can send this off to be cultured and get the correct strain. We also have a hyperbaric chamber. I would like her to start treatments in that."

Sharon raised her eyebrows. "You have that here?"

"We are a top-notch private clinic," Agustin reminded her gently. "I'm going to prep the operating room. I need to clean and debride the wound before the infection spreads and damages any more tissue. Are you feeling up to assisting me in the operating room tonight?"

Sharon nodded. "I can. I feel good. I swear."

"Please page an anesthesiologist. I will get her into surgery after she's had a proper dose of the vancomycin with her penicillin."

"Right away."

Agustin watched Sharon leave to get the lab to culture and find out which strain of Staphylococcus aureus they were dealing with and to start her treatments.

He would send Alondra down to the hyperbaric chamber after the surgery. Necrotizing infections in the soft tissue could spread fast and he needed to get in there and make sure that everything was cleaned up before it did worse damage.

If they let it go too long it could get into her heart and cause endocarditis and kill her. Agustin also wanted to find out how she got this infection and he would have to make sure that everything involving Alondra and this surgery would be sanitized heavily so that no other patient would catch it.

It was a nasty bacterial infection.

He was worried about Sharon being in the operating room with him, especially in her condition, but she was safe. His daughter was safe and Sharon was a capable scrub nurse, when she didn't faint. There was no one else he wanted by his side tonight.

He just wanted her.

Don't faint. Don't faint.

Sharon was repeating that mantra over and over in her head as she scrubbed in to enter the operating room. Other than being a little tired, she felt fine. The nausea was gone, and she didn't have a headache. She actually felt okay today.

When she had a moment after prepping Alondra for her surgical debridement, she took a rest. She got off her feet and made sure she had small snacks and drank lots of fluids. The baby was kicking like crazy. As much as she wanted to revel in every second of that, she didn't have time, but whenever her little girl kicked she thought of that moment in the car when Agustin had asked to touch her belly and he felt that kick too.

His eyes had sparkled in the dim light of the car and then he'd called her *querida* and touched her face, kissing her on top of her head. It was sweet, but in that moment she wanted more than just a peck on the head, she wanted to touch his lips again.

She wanted to feel him and share in that moment of connection between him, her and their little girl. She forgot herself completely in that moment when she kissed him and it turned into something more.

Something she knew couldn't continue, but she wanted it to.

Sharon was glad when he ended the kiss, but since then she noticed that he had put a wall up. There was something eating away at him and she didn't know what. She knew that grief did funny things to people, and even though he didn't have a great relationship with his father he was still grieving him nonetheless, but there was something else that troubled Agustin.

And she didn't know what.

It's not your business.

Only she couldn't shove that thought to the side, because the more time she spent with him and Sandrine, the more and more she wanted to be around him. The more she was liking him and the more her feelings were melting for him.

It had her thinking, briefly in the dark hours of the night alone in her bed, that maybe a relationship wouldn't be a terrible thing. Agustin was a good man—but that meant nothing. Her mother had thought her father was a good man.

Maybe if her mother hadn't died he wouldn't have left because she, a child, reminded him too much of his late wife. So much so he couldn't stand it.

Sharon finished scrubbing up and headed into the operating room. Dr. Nunez the anesthesiologist was there and they were prepping a very terrified Alondra on the table. Sharon was gowned and gloved. She headed over to the patient.

"How are you, Alondra?" she asked gently.

"I'm scared. I was scared during the tummy tuck and I'm scared now." Her voice trembled.

"It's okay. You are in very good hands. Dr.

Varela is one of the best. You will be right as rain."

Alondra nodded. "I shouldn't have gone swimming before we flew down here. That lagoon didn't look right, but Max insisted."

Sharon and Agustin shared a look across the surgical table.

"Brackish water, Alondra?" Sharon asked.

Alondra nodded. "My abuela told me to never swim in water like that. She knew too many people in her village that died from infections after swimming in that water and having an open wound."

"You had a wound?" Agustin asked.

"A paper cut," Alondra said. "I put a plaster on it."

"That wouldn't keep out the bacteria," Sharon said gently. "At least we now know how you got it. Thank you for telling us."

Alondra nodded.

"Now take in a deep breath and count backward from ten," Dr. Nunez said, placing a mask over Alondra's nose.

Alondra began to count backward from ten, but she didn't even make it past the number seven before she was unconscious. Sharon assisted the anesthesiologist as they taped Alondra's eyes shut and inserted a breathing tube down her throat.

Then Sharon was free to assist Agustin on the wound.

"Thankfully, we caught it early enough," Agustin stated. "It could've done so much more damage."

Sharon nodded and handed him the instruments he needed. She didn't want to say much, because she didn't want to overly focus on the surgery. The last time she did that she fainted. Instead she focused on the equipment he needed like sponges to repair the damage, holding the suction when he needed it held.

She winced slightly as the baby began to kick.

"Are you feeling well, Sharon?" Agustin asked, not looking up as he finished the task at hand.

"The baby is kicking and it's making it hard to concentrate. I'm fine though," she said.

Agustin nodded. "Good, we're almost done here. We need to watch her overnight and I would like to continue her regimen of penicillin and vancomycin. Tomorrow afternoon I will instruct staff to place her in the hyperbaric chamber."

"Sounds good." Sharon handed him the suture kit before he asked. He looked surprised, but nodded his appreciation as he finished up with their patient.

When it was all done, Sharon cleaned up and took the instruments off to be sterilized. She was glad that Agustin wanted her to work with him, but there was a part of her that hated this professional distance too, especially after what happened today.

She shook those thoughts from her head.

What she needed to do right now was focus on her work and then go and find a quiet place to curl up before she went to check on Alondra again. Right now, she had to take care of herself first rather than wrestling with the conflicting emotions she was feeling about Agustin and their situation.

Right now, to do her job and to take care of her health, she needed to have a nap.

CHAPTER NINE

SHARON WAS DISAPPOINTED that she and Agustin didn't get to talk right after Alondra's successful treatment of her necrotizing soft tissue infection. Instead, Agustin threw himself into his work and so she did the same.

It was like it was before the ultrasound.

They just seemed to settle into this happy existence of working and going home together. It was like they were neighbors, but then there were some times during the day she would look up from where she was working and she would see his gaze fixed on her, smoldering, just like that night long ago in Barcelona.

It was hunger, but then again she might be wrong, because she was feeling that way about him. Thinking about that night and thinking about their kiss in the car. Just one simple kiss and it enflamed her senses and brought it all right back, sharp into focus. And she wanted more.

So much so, she couldn't stop thinking about it for weeks.

At the time, she was glad he had ended the kiss. Now she wasn't so sure.

It's hormones. That's it. Hormones.

Only she didn't think that was the only thing. She had a feeling that her traitorous heart was falling for him and she wasn't thrilled with that.

It's not what she wanted.

She didn't want a relationship.

She didn't want to start having more than friendly feelings for Agustin and she hated that she was getting used to seeing him around, that he was slowly starting to mesh himself into her life. She worried about what would happen with Sandrine and her abuela if it all came crashing down.

It wasn't only the situation with Agustin that was causing her undo stress. It was the bank in Buenos Aires and this whole legal issue about her abuela's back taxes on that property that was eating away at her. She was going to have to make arrangements with Maria to stay with her grandmother and take some time off work to fly up to Buenos Aires before she got too big to travel and sell the property.

Sharon could feel her cheeks heat and she pulled out her portable blood pressure monitor. She was worrying about this too much today. It was her day off at the clinic and she needed to relax. The last checkup she had with Dr. Perez, her OB/GYN, there had been a slight elevation of proteins in her urine and she was threatening to put Sharon on bedrest. Which was the last thing she needed.

Her aunt always used to say that Sharon tried to solve the world's problems, but never her own.

Maria was puttering about in the kitchen doing some cleaning. Her abuela was moving around well with her walking frame and outside Ushuaia was in a blanket of snow.

"Sandrine will be home soon," Abuela remarked. "I have a new puzzle for us."

Sharon smiled weakly. "That sounds like fun."

Only she couldn't really put any enthusiasm into that thought. Not when she had to get herself to Buenos Aires.

"*Querida*, you're quiet today. Is it the baby?" her abuela asked, coming over to touch her forehead and then her belly.

"I'm okay. Just feeling a little down. I think it's the winter weather. I've been away too long in the northern hemisphere. I'm used to this being my summer."

Not a total lie, but the winter wasn't what was really bothering her.

"Are you sure your blood pressure is fine?" Abuela asked, in a very clear moment.

"Positive," Sharon responded.

She was twenty-seven weeks along and yes, her blood pressure was elevated, but Dr. Perez wasn't overly concerned.

Yet.

"As long as you're sure," Abuela said carefully.

"I might have to go to Buenos Aires for a couple days, Abuela," Sharon blurted out. "As soon as I can make arrangements."

"Why?" her grandmother asked, concerned.

"To sell that property," Sharon stated.

"What property?" Abuela asked.

"Remember the one you thought was sold, but wasn't?"

The one you thought was gone, but your accountant stole that tax money and fled, and it took the government five years to track you down because the accountant had used your name but not your address because the accountant was profiting off it?

Only Sharon didn't say that. It had cost a lot of money to find that information out.

She kept all that to herself, because it would

upset her grandmother, but it ate away at her, made her stomach twist.

Her abuela frowned. "I don't understand."

"Just some business stuff, Abuela," Sharon said, gently because it was easier to calm her grandmother down than agitate her. "I better go now and take care of it before I won't be able to fly."

"I wish you weren't going alone. Maybe ask Agustin to go with you?" her abuela suggested.

"Agustin is my boss, not my boyfriend."

"He's the father of the baby," Abuela stated firmly before wandering away to check on Maria in the kitchen.

Sharon just sighed.

She should let Agustin know where she was going. She pulled out the letter again and stared at it—it made her stomach turn just looking at it.

The last thing she wanted to do was get sick again.

She could tell him why, so he wouldn't worry.

Rely on yourself, a voice reminded her.

Only she didn't want to.

Maybe he'd have some good advice.

She had managed to get her nausea under control for the last month and she was very hopeful that it wouldn't make a comeback, but anytime she thought of something stressful, the sickness returned and her blood pressure rose.

It was decided—she needed to deal with this all now rather than later.

"Maria, can I speak with you?" Sharon said, standing up.

Maria came out of the kitchen. "Of course, what do you need?"

"I have to make arrangements to fly to Buenos Aires for some business before the baby comes. Would you be able to stay overnight with my abuela for a couple of days? I would pay you time and a half of course."

Maria nodded. "That's perfectly acceptable. I can do this weekend?"

Sharon was relieved. "That's great. I will just make arrangements."

Maria nodded. "No problem."

Sharon collected up her purse and grabbed her coat. She needed to go to the clinic and talk to the head nurse in charge of scheduling to let her know what was happening. Talk to Agustin. Then she would go buy a ticket.

"I'll be back in a couple of hours, abuela!" Sharon called out as she headed outside.

It didn't take her long to navigate her way to the clinic and she went straight to the head nurse and asked for the weekend off, explaining she had to take care of some personal business before she got too large to travel.

The nurse in charge of rotation had no issue and Sharon could already feel the stress melting away. She had two hurdles taken care of. She had someone to sit with her grandmother and now had the time off work.

As she was leaving the nursing station she ran straight into Agustin. The moment she saw him, her heart skipped a beat and she could feel her whole body respond to him.

"Sharon, what're you doing here? I thought you had the day off?" he asked, shocked.

"I did, but I came to ask Carmen if I could get some time off," she responded quickly, hoping that would end the conversation.

"You're going on leave?" Agustin asked.

She frowned. "I'm not going on leave. Dr. Perez hasn't said anything to me about going on leave. I have to go to Buenos Aires for a couple of days."

Agustin frowned. "Buenos Aires? Why?"

"That's what I want to talk to you about. Can we talk in private?"

He nodded and led her into a private office and shut the door behind them.

"Tell me," he said.

"My abuela owes back taxes on a property

she thought she'd sold, but she was swindled. We're still trying to figure it all out, but it's mostly sorted, but I need to go to Buenos Aires to sell the property and sign some papers with my lawyer. I'm going to have to sell her house if I can't get a mortgage or work out a deal. I've spent a lot of money dealing with this and selling Abuela's home will help with some mounting legal fees after the property is sold." She handed the letter to him. He read it.

"Back taxes from a property?" he asked.

"*Sí*. So I'm now her power of attorney and I'm going to talk to the bank."

It felt like such a relief to tell him.

"Perhaps I can loan…"

"No," she said, quickly cutting him off. "I can handle this on my own."

He handed her back the letter. "Very well."

"I appreciate the offer, Agustin, but I can manage. I've just got to go to Buenos Aires to meet with an agent and sign papers. After what happened to my abuela, I need to see it through in person."

So she'd know it was all done with and taken care of.

"What about your abuela?" Agustin asked.

"Maria is going to stay with her this weekend."

"You're going to Buenos Aires this weekend?" he asked, stunned.

"Yes. So if you're around, could you check in on my grandmother or at least send Sandrine over?"

Agustin worried his bottom lip. "Actually, I'll be in Buenos Aires this weekend."

"What?" Sharon asked, carefully.

"I've tracked down Sandrine's mother, my stepmother," he said, with an air of contempt.

"Oh," Sharon said. "Does Sandrine know?"

He shook his head. "She does not, but I have to go to Buenos Aires and… Sandrine's mother is signing over her parental rights. To me."

Sharon instantly felt sorry for the young girl and sat down in a chair.

At least Agustin had found Sandrine's mother. No one knew what'd happened to her father.

As far as she knew her father was still wanted on charges of abandonment and endangerment in New York state.

"Oh. That's awful."

"Sí," Agustin said stiffly. "It's why I've been so preoccupied."

"Right. So, you're going to Buenos Aires too. I was just going home to buy my ticket."

"I leave tonight, but I'm staying there until

Monday. I can meet you at the airport when you get in on Friday and take you to your hotel, and perhaps you can meet my mother."

Now Sharon was really shocked. "You want me to meet your mother?"

"*Sí.* She knows about the baby and she's thrilled."

"She knows that we're not together, right?" Sharon asked carefully.

"Of course," he said. "She wants to meet you."

"She's not going to hate me for ruining her son?" Sharon said teasingly.

He shook his head. "Hardly."

"Okay, I would like to meet her. She is our daughter's grandmother."

Agustin smiled and nodded. "Good. I'm glad that's settled. Are you sure I can't help you?"

"I told you, no."

"I see."

"I really have to get to the airport and book my flight."

"Of course, and I have to get back to work." Agustin opened the door. "You have my number, text me when you land on Friday and I will come for you."

"Thank you," she said. Sharon had traveled extensively—she knew how to get a cab and transportation in larger cities. She'd grown up in New York, after all. But she was still appreciative that he would be there. It calmed her to know she would have a familiar face in Buenos Aires, but also she couldn't help but wonder if there was some kind of destiny trying to throw them together.

Agustin sat in his rental car, waiting for Sharon to come out of the airport. It was still winter here, but Buenos Aires was farther north and milder than Ushuaia in the south. It was nice to not worry about snow and this weekend in July it was even warmer than usual. He was glad there was no cold snap.

It would make it safer for Sharon to be here, especially when she was staying at a hotel on her own.

She's a grown woman. She's traveled the world.

Still, he couldn't shake that worry that something could happen to her or the baby. All he could think about was Luisa and getting the call that he had lost her and the baby. All that dread that he'd suffered through came clamoring back and he had to shake it away.

Sharon was not his wife.

She wasn't even his girlfriend. She was just the mother of his child and he had to remind himself of that. But the thing of it was that he had to keep reminding himself of that over and over again lately, because even though he tried to tell himself that their friendship was platonic, the truth was he was falling for her. And it was brutally hard to be falling in love with someone who'd explicitly stated that she wasn't interested in having a relationship.

He was beginning to think of her and her abuela as family. They were forming some kind of tight unit together. It was solidified even more when his stepmother signed over her parental rights.

He was now Sandrine's guardian.

Officially.

Not just her brother.

Agustin sighed thinking about that encounter with his stepmother's attorney. He hadn't even seen the woman and that was probably for the best, but there was a part of him that wanted to ask why she was giving up on her child.

He'd lost a child before and now he couldn't even imagine giving up his unborn daughter.

Maybe they could be a real family. Even if he and Sharon weren't together. She was staying in Ushuaia. Then he remembered her vague answers.

She hadn't confirmed that.

What if Sharon took another job that involved travel again after her abuela died?

It tore his heart out to think of her leaving.

This was why he didn't want a relationship.

It hurt too much.

The car door opened and Sharon popped her head in. "Ah, here you are. I was texting you."

Agustin shook his head clear of all the thoughts running around and around in his mind. He glanced down at his phone, which had unread texts from Sharon. "I'm sorry, I was somewhere else completely. Just zoned right out."

He got out of the car and grabbed her suitcase, putting it into the trunk. Sharon had climbed into the passenger seat. He shut the trunk and got back into the car.

"Did you have a good flight?" he asked.

"Yes. But it was hard to be cramped in a seat for almost four hours and the baby was kicking furiously. The food was awful too."

Agustin chuckled. "Yes. Well, you're here now. Where am I taking you?"

"The hotel Blanca. It's downtown."

Agustin nodded. "I know it well."

He drove away from the airport with a sense of relief that she was here, with him, and he could see that she was safe.

"Did you meet up with your stepmother?" Sharon asked, carefully.

"No. She didn't show up, but her attorney did. She signed over parental rights to Sandrine. Apparently, she's moving to Rio with a new husband and wants a clean break."

Sharon sighed sadly. "Abandoning your kid as a clean break, that's so sad. I should know."

He knew she was thinking of her past and he wanted to comfort her.

He resisted.

"Your father?"

She nodded. "Though my aunt never knew where he went really. Just that she was handed parental rights to me. I don't know if he's dead or alive and I'm not sure I care. He needed a clean break too, I suppose."

"I'm sorry he did that to you. I don't know how I'm going to break it to Sandrine." He sighed.

"If she needs someone to speak to I would be more than happy to talk to her about it," Sharon offered.

His heart warmed. "Would you?"

She nodded. "Yes. Of course. Sandrine is our baby's auntie after all, and it's a role she takes very seriously."

"Yes," Agustin said, smiling. "I'm glad she's been going over to visit your abuela in-

stead of hanging out with that so-called boyfriend she has. That boy is nothing but trouble
and I don't trust him."

"They're just teenagers."

"Exactly," Agustin grumbled.

"Why don't you like him?"

"I don't want Sandrine to make life decisions based on love."

"I get that," she said softly, with a hint of
sadness in her voice.

He didn't want to stress her out or worry
her.

He knew why she was here and he didn't
want to add to it.

"Well, if you don't have plans for dinner
tonight I was thinking I could pick you up
around seven and then we could head over to
my mother's apartment in Recoleta."

Sharon cocked an eyebrow. "Wow, she lives
there?"

"My stepfather is from old Buenos Aires
money."

"Seven?" Sharon asked as Agustin pulled
up to her hotel in the Microcentro.

"*Sí*. I'll wait in the lobby for you."

A porter came up and opened the door for
Sharon. Agustin got out and handed the porter Sharon's suitcase.

"See you then." Sharon waved and the porter followed her into the hotel lobby.

Agustin sighed and got back into his rental. He was staying with his mother and Recoleta, thankfully, was only about twenty minutes away. When he got to the apartment, he parked the car in the underground parking lot. He grabbed his jacket from the back and then noticed the letter had fallen out of Sharon's purse.

He folded the letter up and slipped it into his trouser pocket.

She didn't want him to loan her the money, but her abuela had touched so many lives in Ushuaia.

Maybe she wouldn't turn down help from the community. They could help cover the legal fees?

Maybe it would give her an inkling of home and roots so she wouldn't be tempted to leave.

It was the least he could do for the mother of his child.

You could convince her to stay.

Only he wasn't sure he could. She'd made it clear she didn't want more than a friendly relationship with him.

Against everything his broken heart was telling him, he was falling in love with her.

CHAPTER TEN

AGUSTIN WAITED IN the lobby for Sharon. He was there twenty minutes early and he had the letter safely in his sport coat pocket. When he got a chance, at his mother's, he was going to slip the letter back into her purse.

He had made a few calls. Sandrine was having residents of Ushuaia, in particular their neighborhood, help so that Sharon wouldn't have to move. Their legal fees were high, but people were willing to pitch in to keep Theresa in her home.

He wasn't sure what could be raised, but at least the community was rallying behind Theresa and Sharon. Any little bit would help.

Then Sharon would see you could trust others.

Hopefully, it would allow Sharon to relax and not have to worry about anything. Having her stressed out was not good for the baby and he was sure she was worrying about this. Who wouldn't?

He just wished she'd let him help.

He knew she still didn't fully trust him and borrowing money complicated matters, but he would give it to her, no problem. Still, he understood her misgivings about it.

It was hard to let her through his own barriers.

It was hard to let anyone in.

Agustin heard the elevator ding and glanced over to see Sharon come off the elevator. She was wearing a pink dress. It wasn't the same pink gown that she was wearing the night at the café in Barcelona. This was more of a winter dress, but it was a similar shade of pink, which he thought suited her to perfection. His breath was taken away at the sight of her. Her hair was up in a low chignon. She was stunning and looked flawless.

Graceful.

His blood heated at the sight of her walking toward him and he couldn't help but feel a sense of pride thinking that she was his.

Only she wasn't.

Though there was a part of him that wanted her to be.

Even after all these months since he'd met her and telling himself that his heart couldn't take it, watching her now and knowing that their baby was growing inside her, he wanted her to be his.

Only his.

"You look beautiful," he said.

She blushed. "Thank you. I don't feel very comfortable. I'm really quite nervous."

"There's nothing to be nervous about. My mama loves everyone. She never even hated my father for what he did. She embraced Sandrine as one of her own too and she'll do the same for you."

Sharon smiled shyly. "I hope so. I have never been in this position before, of meeting the parents, probably because I never dated anyone for that long before."

She blushed.

She had said dating.

Are we?

He shrugged it off.

"It'll be fine. Though I remember being nervous meeting Luisa's parents the first time."

The truth slipped out so easily. It was always so hard to talk about Luisa, but it came out and didn't sting as much as it had before.

Agustin wanted to tell her.

"Who is Luisa?" Sharon asked.

"My late wife. I am a widower." It was the first time he was admitting it to her. It was the first time in a long time he had mentioned Luisa to anyone outside his family.

He never talked about her.

Even his partners at the clinic didn't know about her, because he'd met them after Luisa died. All they knew was he was widower. It was always just too painful to think about it and the guilt that ate away at him for not going with her to visit family.

If he'd been with her, then he could've been spared the pain of losing her or could've stopped her.

"You never told me that," Sharon said softly.

"I know. I keep it to myself."

And he did. He and Luisa had lived in Buenos Aires. No one knew she had been pregnant. People in Ushuaia knew how it pained him to talk about his late wife, so they didn't ask questions.

The baby was his secret.

It was easier to keep it all to himself.

"How did she die?" Sharon asked.

He nodded. "She died visiting her family. See, she went on the trip alone. I was too busy to go with her. Work came first."

"You being there might not have changed anything," Sharon replied.

He knew that, but his grief and his guilt over not being there for Luisa told him otherwise. He didn't want to dwell on this anymore. His mother would be anxiously awaiting them and he wanted Sharon and his mother to meet.

"Well, let's go to my mother's. She'll be waiting, probably outside on the street by now, she's that excited."

Sharon nodded, but didn't say anything else. It wasn't how he'd wanted to tell her, but he had been trying to figure out a way to bring it up for some time. It had just come out.

Agustin reached down and took her hand. Sharon didn't pull away, but he could feel her trembling.

"*Querida*, trust me."

Only how could he ask her to trust him, when he was still withholding secrets from her? But he wanted her too.

The more time he spent with her, the more he wanted her to be his, and that was a scary prospect indeed.

Sharon couldn't believe what Agustin had told her.

He had been married and his wife had died tragically. She understood him a bit better now. She understood tragedy.

Although not the kind where you lose the love of your life, and if she had her way she would never.

She knew what grief made some people do.

What it made her father do. At least she thought she did.

There was a niggling worry in the back of her mind that she and their daughter would never be enough for Agustin.

Would the grief over his late wife drive him away like it drove her father away?

Would her daughter be left to the wayside because he was reminded of what he lost before? Or maybe he'd feel like he was betraying his late wife's memory by starting a family with a new woman?

Agustin is not like that.

Sharon ignored that anxious little thought the moment that it crept into her head. She didn't have the space for it now, but she was appreciative that Agustin had shared that with her. It was an odd moment for sure, but she was glad that he had nonetheless.

It also meant that he was beginning to trust her, and maybe she could trust him, even though the idea of doing so was scary. There was a reason she protected her heart.

You're just nervous because you're on your way to a posh neighborhood of Buenos Aires and you're going to meet his mother.

And that was what she had to keep telling herself.

It wasn't the fact that she was falling for Agustin, a man who could very well leave her and her baby. A man who obviously was still grieving his late wife.

It wasn't the fact that the moment she got off the elevator and saw him there in his business casual clothes that her heart beat just a bit faster and she reminisced about their one night together and that kiss they shared a couple of weeks ago.

And it certainly wasn't because when he looked at her it was like she was the only woman in the room. His eyes would sparkle and he would smile only for her.

She was falling for him hard.

This was her first time really falling for someone and it was a terrifying process, but it was exhilarating too.

They didn't say much in the car on the way to Recoleta, but the moment they entered the neighborhood Sharon was in awe at all the French-inspired buildings. It was like she had been transported back to a golden age, when Eva Perón was the first lady and it was all glitz, glamour and romance.

At least that was what Maria, her abuela's care worker, often would say, but Sharon couldn't help feel she romanticized that time period just a bit.

He pulled into an underground car park for one of the larger apartment buildings on the street. As they walked to the elevators, he held out his hand and she took it. It was comforting, his strong hand around hers.

"You're still shaking, *querida*. I told you there's no reason to be nervous."

"No, I'm just knocked up with her son's illegitimate child," Sharon groused.

Agustin chuckled. "That doesn't matter to her, I swear it. Come."

Entering the elevator, he punched in a code and Sharon watched the numbers roll by until they were on the second-to-top floor. The doors opened straight into an art deco and French-inspired apartment.

Sharon gasped at the large floor-to-ceiling windows directly in front of her across the lounge area, looking out on the Atlantic Ocean. She could see all the lights from the boats and the cruise ships glittering in the darkness.

"Oh. wow," Sharon whispered.

"I know, it's something, isn't it?" He took her purse for her and set it down in the entranceway table.

It was at that moment his mama came floating around the corner.

"Agustin, you finally brought her." The

woman was willowy and elegant. Her silver hair was pulled back tight into a bun and her clothes were high-end, and Sharon couldn't help but think that if Eva Perón had aged and was still alive, then Agustin's mother could be her doppelganger.

"Mama, this is Sharon. Sharon, this is my mother, Ava."

Sharon could see where Agustin got his warm, twinkling dark eyes from. Ava smiled, holding open her arms wide and embracing her in a warm hug that caught Sharon a bit off guard.

"It is a pleasure to finally meet you," Ava said, her voice catching. She took a step back and her gaze traveled over Sharon, resting on her bump. "I can't tell you how excited I am that you're making me an abuela. Finally! And that it's a girl!"

"It's a pleasure to meet you too," Sharon said, still a little overcome by the warm welcome. "Thank you for inviting me into your beautiful home."

"Of course! Why don't I give you a tour. It's two floors! Come." Ava grabbed her hand, not taking no for an answer. "Agustin, are you coming?"

"I'll be there shortly, Mama. Show Sharon

around," Agustin said. "Is Javier coming to-night?"

Ava nodded. "Your stepfather will be here soon. He wouldn't miss meeting the mother of his future grandchild! Come, Sharon, I want to show you everything and then I'll take you out on the terrace. It's unseasonably warm this time of year. I still find it cold, but you come from Tierra del Fuego and New York City, so you probably think this is warm!"

Sharon couldn't help but smile around Agustin's mother. She usually didn't like to be led off with strangers in a strange place, but Ava seemed to have this way of just welcoming you. Agustin was right, his mother didn't seem to care one iota that she and Agustin were not married or that her grandchild would be illegitimate.

She was glad that Ava was open-minded.

They walked up a spiral staircase to the second floor. "These are the bedrooms. There are fourteen up here."

Sharon's eyes widened. "Fourteen?"

"Yes. I want to dedicate one of them to the baby, so that when you come visit me with the baby you'll both have your own rooms." Ava stopped in front of a door and opened it. "I'm afraid I got excited and already started decorating, but you can tell me if you don't like it."

Sharon walked into the dimly lit room and was taken aback by the large room that was decorated in soft pastel colors. There was a round crib in the center of the room and a matching change table and dresser. There were also toys, and everything reminded her of a fairy princess kind of dream.

Her eyes filled with tears.

This was too much.

What if things changed and didn't work out?

"If it's too much, I'm sorry. I am an interior decorator and I'm just so excited about this little girl and for you and Agustin. Agustin lost his wife and child, you know, and I know he's always longed for a family."

Sharon's heart stopped for a moment.

His child?

Agustin had told him about his wife, but he hadn't mentioned a child. It broke her heart to think about that kind of pain. She wrapped her arms around her belly. She was giving him what his late wife couldn't. What if he resented her?

What if after all was said and done she couldn't give him what he'd lost?

"I love it, Ava," Sharon said, choking back tears. "It's beautiful and very generous."

Ava beamed happily. "Oh, I'm so glad you like it."

"Mama, the caterer has questions," Agustin said, coming into the room.

"Oh, okay. I'll be back. Show her around the rest of the place, Agustin." Ava hurried away and Agustin stepped into the dimly lit room—there were no light fixtures set up yet.

"I'm sorry she went a bit overboard. She does that sometimes," Agustin said.

"Are you okay with this?" she asked.

"Why wouldn't I be?" Yet there was something in his voice that let her know this was hard for him.

She turned to look at him. "Why didn't you tell me about your other child?"

"What?" he asked, choking back emotion.

"Your mother told me."

He sighed and ran his fingers through his hair. "It's too painful."

"I'm so sorry she did this. Are you okay?"

"I told her to. I want our child to feel welcome here. I won't lie, it was hard, but I did pick out some things."

"Like what?" she asked, curious at his hand in this nursery.

Agustin walked over and picked up a doll. It reminded her of the doll she had when she was abandoned.

He handed it to her and she gingerly held it against her chest.

"It's lovely." The tears flowed down her cheeks.

She felt like she didn't deserve this.

She didn't deserve any of it.

"*Querida,*" Agustin said, gently closing the distance between them. He wrapped her up in his arms and held her. "Don't cry."

"I should be comforting you. No wonder work is your life."

Agustin nodded. "It was ten years ago. She was pregnant, just newly pregnant so I didn't even know if the baby was a boy or a girl, but it crushed me. I didn't think that I would ever have children. Not sure I wanted them to be honest."

"And now?"

Agustin smiled and tipped her chin. "Well, now it can't be helped. No tears. Please don't feel sorry for me. We need to take care of you and our little girl, yes?"

Sharon nodded, swallowing the lump in her throat, but there was a part of her that couldn't shake her heartache over Agustin and his loss. She couldn't even begin to fathom the pain of losing a child. Or the fear he might change his mind and leave because the grief was too much.

Because she reminded him of his late wife, and their daughter of the child he never got to hold.

Her baby kicked in her belly.

Agustin chuckled.

"What?" she asked.

"I felt that." He was grinning and reached down to touch her belly. "Maybe she's hungry?"

Sharon laughed softly. "Maybe. I am."

"Then let's go downstairs. Javier has arrived and I'm sure the appetizers are out. Apparently a couple of old family friends are coming tonight too to meet you. It's quite the party my mother organized. I'm sorry, I had no idea. I just knew about this room."

Sharon wiped the tears on the back of her hand. "It's okay. We can socialize. Your mother is so sweet. I think I can manage this for her."

Agustin grinned and held out his hand. "Good, because there is no escaping now."

She laughed and took his hand. It felt like it was natural, like it was the right thing to do as he led her from that beautiful nursery and down to meet a bunch of strangers. The problem was, all she could think about was Agustin and his pain.

She remembered her father's pain clearly. It haunted her.

It all made sense to her now, and in this moment all she wanted to do was comfort him and assure him that everything would be okay.

Their baby was fine.

They would be okay, provided she was able to talk to the bank tomorrow and work out some kind of arrangement for the legal fees. At least the property in Buenos Aires would be up for sale soon. She was dealing with a reputable Realtor.

Sharon had met with them after she checked in. The property in question was run-down and she wasn't sure if there would be anything left over after the sale and the taxes to pay the legal fees she racked up. She was still pretty sure they would have to sell her abuela's home in Ushuaia.

It didn't sound like Agustin ever wanted to take another chance on love, and it was all well and good to have a beautiful nursery in someone else's home, but Sharon had learned at an early age that the only person you could rely on was yourself.

And for that reason, she had to make sure Abuela and her were taken care of if Agustin ever thought their presence in his life was too painful.

Her heart was already breaking, because in spite of all this, she was falling for him.

CHAPTER ELEVEN

SHARON HAD A lovely dinner with Agustin's parents Ava and Javier and their friends.

She tried to forget, though, the niggling thoughts in the back of her mind about Agustin's loss.

It reminded her of her childhood and her father's grief and the abandonment.

Then there was the nursery and the doll he bought for their daughter.

It meant so much to her, but she was still completely overwhelmed. There was a part of her that thought maybe she could have a happily-ever-after, after all.

And yet, it was hard to believe.

She hated the fact she had become so indecisive. What was happening to her?

Love? a little voice suggested, but she shook that thought away. There was no way it could be that. She was vigilant about keeping the idea of love out of her heart.

After dessert Agustin discreetly excused them, much to her relief, and took her back to her hotel. She thanked him for a wonderful night and they made arrangements to meet for lunch after her appointment at the bank.

She should say no, but it would be nice to see him because she wasn't looking forward to talking to the bank tomorrow.

What she needed was a good night's sleep. The problem was that she didn't get that. All night long she thought about the bank appointment as well as Agustin's loss.

She was worried he'd be so torn up with memories that he would leave her and the baby behind to escape the ghosts of his past.

She also hated that this was keeping her up all night.

She didn't have time to think about this.

She needed rest.

Then the pain hit her. Hard. In the center of her back and tightening around her front.

Oh. God.

She rolled over and grabbed her phone, calling Agustin and hoping that he was awake.

"Querida?" he asked, confused.

"Something is wrong. I'm having…pain and tightening."

"The baby?"

"Sí," she said as another wave hit her.

"I'm on my way. I'll be there in fifteen minutes."

"Hurry. I'm going to call the concierge for an ambulance."

"I'll call an ambulance. Stay put."

"Okay," Sharon said, through another bout of pain. She was trying to think of all the things it could be, but through the pain she couldn't rationalize any options. She had spent all her career using that calm, logical mind to help patients.

Right now, with her baby on the line and pain coming in waves, she couldn't think of what it could be.

She wasn't sure how long she was lying there for, but it wasn't too much longer until Agustin and the hotel manager were opening her door. She let out a cry of relief as Agustin came to her side, and behind the hotel manager she could see an ambulance crew.

"Querida?" Agustin asked softly. He was kneeling beside her, stroking her face gently.

"It feels like contraction, but it shouldn't be a contraction. It's too early."

Agustin didn't try to tell her that she might be foolish. Instead he helped her sit up and the paramedics took over.

He fired off instructions to the paramedics on which hospital to take her to and then never left her side. Sharon held his hand as she was wheeled out of her hotel room and into the waiting ambulance downstairs.

Agustin climbed into the back of the ambulance with her, never letting her go and holding on to her.

"Thank you," she said over the sirens as they made their way through Buenos Aires.

"For what?" he asked.

"Staying with me."

He smiled and caressed her face. "Where else would I be?"

She didn't want to think about where else he could be, because the important thing in this moment was he was here with her right now.

Agustin wasn't allowed in the room when the obstetricians on call were examining Sharon. Just like what happened in Ushuaia.

He wasn't her husband and even though he was the father, it didn't seem to matter. Sharon hadn't told anyone he was allowed to go in, so therefore he had to wait outside. It also didn't matter that he was Dr. Varela. His name and reputation as a plastic surgeon, a world-renowned one at that, didn't matter in the least. It was a bit maddening.

He was sent to the waiting room on the obstetrical floor and all he could do was pace.

He also hated this. He was a doctor and he was used to being on the other side of the curtain, as it were. It also reminded him of a different waiting room.

One where he was alone.

Waiting on the status of his wife, but knowing that she was already gone when they put him in a private waiting room.

Here, there were others.

He wasn't alone, but all those old feelings came rushing back to him. The moment that Sharon had called him, frantic, telling him that she was scared, well, it'd sent an ice-cold shiver of dread through him.

He was glad that he was there with her and this hadn't happened when he was in Buenos Aires and she was in Ushuaia.

If something had happened to her or the baby in Ushuaia while he'd been here, he never would've forgiven himself. He couldn't bear it if he lost another child. Another woman he cared for.

Agustin glanced at the clock on the wall.

It had been three hours since Sharon had been brought in.

What is taking so long?

"Dr. Varela?" a doctor questioned, sticking his head into the room.

"Sí." Agustin made his way over to him.

"Miss Misasi is doing fine. She was not in labor. It was Braxton Hicks, they were particularly strong though and we are concerned that her blood pressure was slightly elevated, but it has come down. I think it was due to the stress of the contractions."

"Braxton Hicks. Well, that's good news," Agustin said, relieved.

"She's going to be discharged, but I would like her to rest today and I don't want her to be on her own. Would you be able to stay with her?" the doctor asked.

"Of course. I will take care of her and I will take her back to Ushuaia myself. That is if it's okay to travel?"

The doctor nodded. "She was very vexed about being admitted. She explained about her grandmother. I would like her to rest for a couple of days before she flies home."

"That makes sense, and I'll make arrangements for her grandmother so she won't worry about that," Agustin said.

The doctor nodded. "Very good, Dr. Varela. You can go in and see her now and take her back to her hotel."

Agustin shook the doctor's hand and made his way to the room that Sharon was in. She would not like the idea of remaining in Buenos Aires for a couple of extra days, but it was doctor's orders. He would call Maria himself and make sure she was compensated well, and there was Sandrine to stay with Sharon's abuela at night.

He would tell Sandrine what was happening.

Sandrine already knew about the situation with Sharon's abuela. He knew he would have to ease her worry about the bank. The bank could wait. Right now all that mattered was her health and the baby's health.

"Come in," Sharon called out.

Agustin opened the door. "I'm told I can take you back to the hotel."

Sharon sighed. "I feel kind of foolish right now."

"Why?" he asked.

"Braxton Hicks. I know what those are." She rubbed her abdomen. "I really know what those are now."

Agustin chuckled. "It's different when it's you going through them and not in a textbook."

She nodded. "He wants me to stay in Buenos Aires, but my abuela…"

"All taken care of, or will be. I will handle arrangements and you can fly back to Ushuaia with me on Monday."

"That's too kind, but I really can't have you stepping in like this."

"And why not? We're friends, coworkers and neighbors. We also share a baby who is the reason you're being afflicted right now."

Sharon smiled, her eyes twinkling. "I suppose so."

"You suppose nothing. I'm right, aren't I?"

"Okay, but I have a meeting with a bank. I am here for things regarding my abuela's property."

"When we get back to the hotel you can call your lawyers and tell them what happened. If you feel up to it on Monday we'll reschedule the meeting. No one will blame you for missing it due to health reasons. Right now, you need to rest so we can get you back to Ushuaia."

Sharon looked mollified. "You're right."

"Of course I am." He grinned.

The nurse came in, bringing the discharge forms. Sharon signed them and a wheelchair was brought into her room.

"Normally, I would object to a wheelchair, but as I don't have my shoes, I think I'll ride in this."

Agustin smiled. "A taxi is downstairs waiting for us as I left my car at your hotel."

"Thanks again for coming with me."

"You need to stop thanking me. This is my baby too."

Sharon climbed into the wheelchair. Agustin took Sharon out to the waiting cab. He scooped her up in his arms and carried her to the vehicle.

"You're being ridiculous." Sharon chuckled.

He grinned. "Just taking care of my…"

"Your what?" she asked quietly.

He didn't know what to say. She wasn't his wife, and she wasn't his girlfriend.

The woman you're falling in love with?

"The mother of my child," he quickly said.

"Oh." She looked slightly disappointed, but it was a fleeting expression. "Right."

He climbed in beside her in the back of the cab and gave the driver instructions on where to go. When they got to the hotel he carried her into the lobby. They made it back up to her room with the help of a spare keycard, as hers was inside the room with her purse.

It was four in the morning and now the adrenaline was wearing off.

He was tired.

Sharon made her way to the bed and climbed in under the covers.

"You look exhausted," she said.

"I am. Are you hungry? Do you want room service?" he asked.

"No. Just sleep."

"Sounds good," he said, relieved. He made his way over to the chair in the corner.

"What're you doing?" she asked.

"Sleeping. The doctor at the hospital doesn't want you to be alone."

"I know that. What I mean is why are you sleeping there? This is a king bed. You can sleep next to me." She patted the empty spot.

His pulse thrummed. The last time they shared a bed no sleeping had happened.

"Are you sure?" he asked, looking at the bed longingly, but worried about the implications.

"Of course. That chair can't be comfortable."

"No. It's not." He got up and climbed on top of the blankets lying on his back. Now, lying here in bed with her, he wasn't as tired as he had been. He was more terrified of giving in to how his body was reacting being in bed with her.

Being so close to her again. He could just reach out and touch her. She wasn't just some random memory that he had been clinging to since their night in Barcelona.

She was here. So why didn't he reach out to her?

Agustin rolled onto his side and he could hear the even breathing of her in sleep.

It hadn't taken her long to fall asleep and he was glad for that.

He closed his eyes and tried to resist the pull of snuggling closer to her. He resisted the urge to hold her in his arms. The urge to make her his. Like he wanted to.

He woke with a start when he felt the mattress move.

He saw Sharon pacing by the window. She had changed and it looked like she'd had a shower.

"What's wrong?" he asked groggily.

"Sorry, did I wake you?" Her voice sounded agitated.

"It's fine. Are you okay?"

"Yes. I'm fine."

"What time is it?" he asked.

"One in the afternoon."

Agustin balked. "One?"

It felt like he'd hardly slept at all. He hadn't dreamed and he felt even more tired than usual.

"I woke up at eleven. Talked to my attorney then had a shower to figure out some things." She worried her bottom lip.

"Is everything okay?" he asked.

"Yes," she murmured. "I'll talk to a Realtor when we get back."

"You don't have to," he said.

"I can't get a mortgage for Abuela's house and the sale of the property will be a loss. It was in shambles. The legal fees I had to pay… I tried to get an appeal on the taxes as she'd been swindled, but unless I spend more money to track down the thief and wait for his extradition…" She sighed. "This is just easier. I sell Abuela's house and I find a more affordable place."

"But I can help."

"No," she said softly. "I can't let you do that, Agustin."

"Why?" He wanted to know. He wanted to help her. He wanted to be there for her and it was hard to have her push him away.

"It's something I have to do."

He understood that. He didn't like it, but he understood it.

"Are you hungry?" he asked, changing the subject.

"Yes. Starving."

"Okay. I'll clean up and we'll go out since your business has been taken care of. The doctor wants you to stay until Monday and your abuela's care has been arranged, so now we'll have some fun."

"Fun?" she asked in disbelief. "Not sure I

know the meaning of that. Last time I let loose and had fun I ended up pregnant."

He chuckled. "Well, I can't get you any more pregnant than you are, so we'll just have a nice time."

Sharon shook her head, but was smiling. "Okay, but hurry up. I'm hungry and I'm buying since you're staying with me."

"Right away, Nurse." He headed into the bathroom to have a quick shower and freshen up. He would have to stop by his mother's place and grab his clothes. He'd let his mother know what was going on and she would insist on him staying with her.

And Agustin was glad that Sharon seemed to be in better spirits. Maybe now she would relax, and that was the goal for today. To help her de-stress, which he hoped would keep his mind off wanting to help her relax in a completely different way by staying put in bed.

Sharon was glad for the distractions. She needed some light and happiness, especially after last night and talking to her lawyers this morning.

She had been so scared and then felt absolutely foolish for not recognizing Braxton Hicks contractions. She was thankful for Agustin though, and that he'd come to take care of her. It was nice to have him there soothing her, telling her it would be okay and holding her.

She was a strong, independent woman, but she liked he'd been there last night, and she'd slept so calmly with him next to her. It had felt right.

Like she belonged by his side.

It was nice to depend on someone, but it was something she couldn't get used to. The only person she could rely on was herself.

As much as she wished she could take him up on his offer to help, she couldn't.

It wasn't right.

They weren't together and what would happen if he changed his mind?

She'd be left with nothing.

It was better that she handled it.

She had a lot to do when she got back to Ushuaia. The doctor at the hospital had made it clear that he didn't want her stressed out.

Agustin had made that clear too.

And it might be nice to have some fun. Enjoy a mild winter's day in Buenos Aires.

Agustin took her to a café that overlooked the water and they talked about his mother and her friends. There was just an ease to their conversation. It was light and it felt like they had been talking this way for a long time.

After their late lunch they decided to go for a walk downtown. The sun was shining and it was almost warm out. It felt like a spring day in New York City.

"Sandrine just texted that it's snowing in Ushuaia," Agustin groused.

"Did you rub it in that it's light jacket weather here?" she said with a smile.

"Why would I rub that in?" he asked.

"You're her older brother. That's what brothers do…apparently."

"Well, I'm more like her father now," he said sadly.

"Good practice for you," she remarked, touching her belly.

"Yes," he said. "Especially when it comes to boys. Sandrine is still seeing that boy I don't trust."

"Diego, you mean. Not *that boy*," she corrected.

He grunted. "Whatever."

"I still don't know why you don't like him. He seems nice enough."

Agustin shook his head. "I know what he wants with her."

Sharon chuckled. "You've got to be fair with her or you'll drive Sandrine away."

He grumbled. "I suppose."

"I guess…" She trailed off as her gaze

landed on a group of teenage boys skateboarding. One of them was skateboarding down a set of steps, specifically the railing part of the steps. She knew what was going to happen before the boy did. He was flung high into the air and landed smack down on his face. Blood pooled under him.

"Good Lord." Agustin raced over as the boy's friends formed a stunned circle around him.

Sharon knelt down to the unconscious boy and checked his ABCs. His airway, breathing and it was clear his C for circulation had failed. The boy was bleeding profusely.

"I need a towel," Agustin shouted, turning to his friends. "Or a T-shirt."

"Here," a boy said, handing him a towel. "Are you a doctor?"

"I am. Do you have a cell phone?" Agustin asked.

The unconscious boy's friend nodded. "Yeah."

"Call an ambulance." As soon as Agustin said that they all ran away.

"What in the word?" Sharon asked, stunned.

"Drugs," Agustin murmured. "I can smell it on him."

"Oh, no."

Agustin handed her the towel. "Hold pressure to his wound and I'll call the ambulance."

Sharon applied pressure on the boy's head wound while Agustin called for an ambulance, then he checked to see if the boy had identification. He did not.

There was nothing. They didn't know who he was or who he belonged to. The boy was alone.

Sharon was heartbroken.

"We can't leave him," she said quietly.

"No. You're right. We'll follow the ambulance then," Agustin said.

The ambulance came and took over. Agustin and Sharon followed the ambulance to a different hospital than she had been take to the previous night. The hospital had an overflowing emergency room. The emergency doctors let Agustin in as they were so overrun, and the boy was alert by the time he was being rolled into a trauma room. After a nurse took his blood to check for illegal drugs and do a CBC panel, the boy was left alone.

He was conscious and therefore not a priority at the moment.

Agustin leaned over the boy. "*Hola*, what is your name?"

"Pedro Gonsalves," the boy answered.

"That's good you remember who you are," Sharon said gently.

"Pedro, do you remember what happened?" Agustin asked.

"No, but my head hurts," Pedro whined.

"Pedro, do you have parents we can contact?" Sharon asked.

"Yes." Pedro gave his number to a nurse who came in with some painkillers for him. The nurse was going to contact his parents.

The ER doctor came in. "Are you his parents?"

"No," Sharon said. "Witnesses. His parents are being called."

"I'm Dr. Varela," Agustin said, stepping forward. "We were on the scene."

The ER doctor was impressed. "Dr. Varela the plastic surgeon?"

"Sí." Agustin nodded at Sharon. "This is Nurse Misasi."

"He's lucky you both were there," the ER doctor said as he examined the boy. "Most likely a mild concussion. I'll send a nurse in to do the sutures. Tox screen shows a low dose of marijuana."

The ER doctor left and they waited for a nurse to come and repair the scalp laceration.

"How old are you, Pedro?" Sharon asked.

"Sixteen," Pedro replied.

"You know you shouldn't do drugs and skateboard. You could've died," Sharon gently chastised him.

"I know," he sighed. "It was foolish. Thanks for helping me."

"Of course. I'm a nurse. It's what I do."

The nurse arrived and went to work stitching up the boy's head wound. A pressure bandage had just been placed on Pedro's head when his parents came in. Agustin spoke to them and they both thanked him profusely.

"Well, not the most relaxing after-lunch walk," Agustin stated as he and Sharon left the hospital.

"No, but I do like watching you work."

"You know, I'm glad you were there with me," he said.

"Are you?"

Agustin nodded. "When we work together… it's like you're an extension of me. I can't explain it. You're so talented."

She could feel the blush in her cheeks. The warmth. It meant so much he valued her work. That he liked working with her. She wasn't used to compliments like that.

"I am bit tired," she responded, steering the conversation away from compliments.

"Let's go back to the hotel." He said it so

easily, almost like saying, *Let's go back home*, and it made her heart skip a beat.

"I could use a nap."

"Me too." Agustin reached down and took her hand. It sent a zing of pleasure through her. He made her feel warm and secure. She wanted to hold on to the moment for as long as she could.

For the first time she was contemplating the idea of relying on someone, of falling in love with someone, but she was too scared to ever really give in to that thought.

She was scared of all the things she was feeling about him and all the things she wanted.

CHAPTER TWELVE

THEY GOT BACK to the hotel and both climbed
into bed. Only now, being in bed with him,
she couldn't sleep. All that exhaustion she
was feeling vanished. Agustin lay there on
his back, with his eyes closed and his hands
folded across his chest.

"I feel like you're watching me," he murmured.

"I'm not."

Only she was. She couldn't help it.

She was falling for him, even though she
didn't want to admit it. Something she never
thought she'd do. She should try to stop herself, but it was hard to. There was a part of
her that didn't want to stop this rush of feelings she was having for him.

There was a part of her that wanted a happily-ever-after. Even if she didn't quite believe
in them still.

Agustin rolled over. "I thought you were tired?"

"I am." She grinned. "I didn't thank you."

"For what?" he asked.

"Taking care of me last night."

"Of course, *querida*. Why wouldn't I take care of you?" he asked, astonished.

"We made no promises that night," she whispered.

"Things have changed."

"Have they?" she asked.

"Haven't they?" he asked back. "You trust me, enough to call me when you need help."

"It's hard to trust. Especially after my father left."

"I'm not your father."

"I know." Although she couldn't completely trust him. Yet she couldn't stop thinking about him. Any walls she put up to protect her heart would come crashing down.

He was the only man ever to get through her defenses.

It would kill her when he left, because it was hard not to think of him staying, but maybe he could change his mind. Maybe she could convince him to stay and that little secret dream of having a family of them, the baby, Abuela and Sandrine in Ushuaia would become a reality.

She could have the family she'd always dreamed of.

Maybe they both needed something worth fighting for.

She leaned in and kissed him like she had before. Gently, but then she wanted to feel all those same feelings she had felt back in Barcelona when she had surrendered to his charms. When she was vulnerable to him.

And she wanted that same vulnerability again. She desired Agustin like no other man.

If this wasn't going to last, she wanted one more night of passion with him.

She deepened the kiss, pulling him close to her, pressing her body against his. Agustin's hands skimmed over her, causing her body to tingle in anticipation.

"Querida," Agustin mumbled against her neck. "When you kiss me like that I lose control."

"I know. I want you too."

Agustin kissed her again. "Are you sure?"

She nodded. "I want you, Agustin. Just like I did in Barcelona. I just want to be with you. Here. Now."

Agustin kissed her all over, his hands over her body as they hastily removed their clothes. Her skin was on fire, wanting to be touched by him. Her blood was singing. Soon it was just them, nothing between them, just their bodies pressed together, skin to skin.

Warmth spread through her, melting her right down to her toes and making her wet with need. His lips trailed over her sensitive skin, down her body to her breasts. Sharon cried out as his tongue swirled around the peak of her sensitive nipples.

Every bit of her reacted to his touch, his tongue. Her body remembered the way he felt under her fingers. The strength of his muscles, the power of his hands on her and the erotic hold he had on her.

She remembered him.

As he nipped at her neck his hand slipped between her legs, stroking her folds, bringing her so close to a climax she arched her hips in response. Her body aching with the need for him to be buried deep inside her.

She wanted all of Agustin.

She wanted more.

So much more.

"What do you need, *querida*?" he whispered against her neck. "Tell me what you want."

"You," she said breathlessly.

Their gazes locked as he entered her. She cried out in bliss.

"Am I hurting you?" he asked.

"No. Don't stop." Sharon didn't want him to stop. She wanted more.

So much more.

She wanted him always, but she knew that was a folly and the pain she felt later would be her fault for letting him in and loving him.

Right now, she didn't care about any of that.

Right now Sharon wanted Agustin deeper. She wrapped her legs around his waist, begging him to stay, wanting him pressed against her, which was impossible because of her belly.

"*Querida*, let's try another way." Agustin pulled out. "Lie on your side."

Sharon obeyed. He took her leg and draped it over him as he entered her from behind.

"Touch yourself," he whispered in her ear. "I want to feel you come around me."

Sharon began to stroke her clitoris. Her body lighting up as pleasure washed over her.

Agustin quickened his pace as she came around him, heat scorching through every fiber, every cell in her body.

It wasn't long before Agustin came. She was in a pile of goo as he eased her leg down, kissing her shoulder.

"*Querida*," he whispered.

Sharon wanted to tell him that she was in love with him. That she wanted him to stay with her. That she wished he wouldn't go.

Only she couldn't say those words because she was so scared of trusting him and her heart enough.

Agustin just lay there after she fell asleep. He was still curled up against her back and he had his hand on her belly, gently caressing her and feeling each little kick from his daughter. He hadn't felt this happy in a long time.

Not since Luisa, and he never thought he would ever feel this way again.

It was unnerving.

And he was scared, but still there was nowhere he would rather be. Just lying with her and feeling his baby kick. His eyes stung with tears, but he quickly swallowed the lump in his throat. He wasn't sure that he deserved to be this happy.

He wasn't sure that he deserved this second chance with a beautiful woman like Sharon. He got up slowly, as to not disturb her, but she rolled in his direction, reaching out.

"Agustin?" she asked sleepily.

"I'm just going to my mother's to get my bag. Go back to sleep, I'll be back in an hour."

"Promise? You're not leaving?"

His heart melted and he kissed her gently on the top of her head. "I will be back."

Sharon didn't open her eyes. Just nodded

and slept, her brown hair fanning across the pillow again. Just like he remembered. Her body tangled in the sheets, but she was shivering so he took an extra blanket from the hotel closet and covered her up, tucking her in, and then kissed her on the cheek.

It was almost like he had been doing it for some time.

Except he hadn't.

He got dressed and grabbed the extra key card. He made his way to his car and took the short drive over to his mother's apartment in Recoleta.

When he got into his mother's place, she was up and pacing. Instantly, the hair stood on the back of his neck.

"What is it?" he asked.

"Oh, I was just about to text you when I saw you come into the lobby. There's been an accident in Ushuaia," his mother said, her voice shaking.

It was like he was in some kind of parallel universe. Has he been transported back in time? "What do you mean?"

"Sandrine, she was in a car accident, from a landslide. She's in the hospital. That's all I know, that's all they'd tell me because you're her legal guardian. They called here looking for you."

Sandrine had been alone. He was doing what he had done to Luisa when he'd worked so much. He felt terrible and knew that they had to get back to Ushuaia as soon as possible.

"I have to take Sharon with me. She's supposed to stay in Buenos Aires since her Braxton Hicks scare, but her abuela will be alone now."

"Maria is with her abuela, I checked," Ava said. "Sharon's abuela was my midwife. I still keep in touch with her."

"Of course you do." Agustin smiled. Theresa was in everyone's life. Maybe it was supposed to be that way.

"You need to take my private jet," Javier, his stepfather, said. "I made a call."

"Thank you, Javier." And he was grateful. He needed to get to Sandrine. It was eating away at him that he hadn't been there again.

What kind of brother was he?

The worst.

If he couldn't be there for Sandrine, how could he be there for his own daughter? It was a terrifying prospect. It chilled him to his very core.

Javier nodded. "Go to Ushuaia and take care of your family."

Agustin just nodded.

His family?

They weren't a family. They were… He didn't know what they were, but family? Did he deserve a family when he couldn't even take care of Sandrine? He had left her alone and she'd been in a car accident and he didn't even know her status.

He was failing.

Again.

Sharon slept on the plane. He hated to wake her up, but when he told her that Sandrine was in the hospital after a car accident, she got up and packed her things. He didn't say much to her as he drove the rental car to the airport where Javier's private plane was waiting.

Once they were settled the pilots got clearance, and when they were in the air Sharon curled up in her seat, her head against the window, and slept.

He wished he could sleep.

It was three-hour flight, in good weather, but all he could think about was how he had failed his sister. He had guardianship over her until she was eighteen, but did he really deserve that? He shouldn't have left her in Ushuaia. He should've brought her to Buenos Aires, but Sandrine had been so insistent on staying in Ushuaia for school and for Sharon's grandmother Theresa.

Sandrine thought of Sharon and her grandmother as family already and he wished that he had that same kind of optimism. He was struggling to connect with his sister too, but the thought of losing Sandrine was too much to bear.

He had issues with his father and didn't have a good relationship with Sandrine's biological mom, but Sandrine was his sister. Besides his mother and Javier, he had no one.

You have Sharon.

Only he didn't. She wasn't his and he was terrified to reach out and make her his, because the idea of losing her the same way that he'd lost Luisa was almost too much to bear.

Yet when he took her in his arms, when he was with her, he wasn't scared.

But in this harsh reality of accidents, the thought of losing Sharon was too much to bear.

"You should head straight home," Agustin said as they collected their luggage.

"No, I'm a nurse. If it's a multi-vehicle accident they'll need all the help they can get," Sharon stated.

"You really think you should be working?" he asked tensely.

"I'm fine."

Agustin was frustrated. "You need rest."

"I'm going." She crossed her arms and there was no point in arguing with her.

They went to the emergency room. It was full and Dr. Reyes, who was Agustin's friend and head of the emergency room, appeared relieved when he caught sight of him.

"Agustin! Sandrine is in room three, but if you can spare some help we have a lot of injured here and a lot of burn victims."

"Of course," Agustin said. "I just need to check on my sister."

"Room three, down the hall," Dr. Reyes said.

"I'm a nurse, a registered practice nurse. Can I help?" Sharon asked.

"Of course," Dr. Reyes replied enthusiastically.

Agustin paused. He wanted to stop her, but she wouldn't listen to him. She wasn't his. There was nothing he could do as she walked off with Dr. Reyes. He wanted to tell her to be careful. Only the words didn't come.

She wasn't his.

Agustin took a deep breath and headed to room three. His heart was hammering as he entered the room. Sandrine was lying there, staring at the walls, her arm bandaged up.

"Sandrine?" he asked tentatively.

She startled and her eyes widened. "Agustin? You came back?"

"Why wouldn't I?" Agustin asked. "I'm your brother, right?"

Sandrine's eyes filled with tears. "No one ever comes for me. Except Father, but he's been gone... I've been so alone."

She began to sob and Agustin took his sister in his arms, holding her.

"It's okay, I'm here," he reassured her.

Sandrine clung to him, crying herself out. Agustin just held her. He was glad she was alive and angry at himself for not being there, for being just as guilty for letting her be alone as her biological mother had done. He was mad at himself for putting his work first, like he did with Luisa and thinking Sandrine needed space.

"I'm here now," Agustin said. "What happened?"

"I was driving with Diego—"

"I knew that boy Diego would get you into trouble."

Sandrine pulled away. "Diego didn't cause the landslide. That's what caused the accident. He pulled me from the burning car."

Agustin felt awful. "Where is he?"

Sandrine's eyes welled with tears. "I don't know. He went to help the others, the cars that were buried."

"Why were you driving with him?"

"Taking the money we raised for Theresa to the bank. We were coming back. We almost raised enough to pay those legal fees."

"What?" Sharon asked.

Agustin spun around to see Sharon standing in the doorway, her arms folded. She looked confused and hurt.

"Sharon? I thought you were helping Dr. Reyes?" he asked.

"I am, but I decided to see Sandrine before I changed into scrubs. What do you mean money was raised for my abuela?"

"The community raised the funds," he said.

"Not the full amount," Sandrine piped up. "Enough that you don't have to move."

Sharon was still confused. "I don't understand."

"You didn't want my help," Agustin stated.

"No. I don't want charity either." Her voice was raised.

He glanced back at Sandrine. "Can we speak in the hall? Sandrine, I'll be back. Rest."

Sandrine shook her head and rolled her eyes as Agustin ushered Sharon out into the hall. He closed the door behind him.

"So you told the community about Abuela's financial troubles?" Sharon asked.

"I did. Theresa needed help. As did you."

"You had no right," she snapped. "That was too much. I have money…"

"Not enough. You were going to sell the home. Move away."

"Only across the city. I'm not poor. It was for me to take care of."

"What does it matter? I took care of it. It was a way for me to help."

"Help? You mean a way to ease your conscience when you leave us eventually."

He knew she was lashing out because she was afraid.

"You're the one leaving by moving away," he countered.

"I'm not really. I'm moving across the city," she said quietly. "You can still see us."

"You don't sound so sure," he snapped. "What happens when your abuela, God forbid, dies and you go back to your old job as a traveling nurse?"

"What happens when you feel guilty about moving on from your grief and leave us?" she asked, trembling. "Just like my father."

"I'm not your father."

"I'm sorry your wife died, but you can't run from your problems."

That struck a painful chord with him. "Look who's talking. You took a job where you never settled. You were running from your pain just as much as I was."

Sharon's lip trembled. "I'm here now and you're abandoning us."

"I am not. You are leaving me by pushing me away, not allowing me to help," he said hotly.

"I'm not."

"Then let it go. Let's leave this all behind and you can accept the money."

"I can't," she whispered.

"What're you afraid of?" he asked.

They didn't say anything for a moment. Just stared at each other. He could see the hurt and anger in her eyes.

He'd put it there.

"I will pay you back, everyone back," Sharon replied coldly.

She turned to leave.

"I'm not your father. I'm not leaving you. You're choosing to leave me."

She looked back over her shoulder. "And I am not your wife, and I'm safe here. I won't have my child left behind. I won't allow her to feel that pain."

He stood there shaking as he let her walk away.

He went back into Sandrine's room, but she was obviously angry with him too.

"Did you make it right?" Sandrine asked.

Agustin ran his hand through his hair and sighed. "It's complicated."

"No. It's not. You love her. I know you do. I was only small when Luisa died, but she would want you to be happy, Agustin."

"I may love Sharon, but she doesn't love me. If she did, she'd trust me."

"Her love is predicated on that?" Sandrine asked. "Seriously. How immature."

"What?" Agustin asked.

Sandrine cocked an eyebrow. "And how do you know she doesn't love you? Just because she is struggling to trust after her trauma? You are too by the way."

Agustin was stunned. "You know about that?"

Sandrine nodded. "She told me. I was struggling with abandonment too. You were always working and…it was a lot."

Agustin pulled her close. "I'm sorry you were struggling, and that I didn't notice."

"You bury your grief in work. It was hard for me to trust you with you putting your work first, but that doesn't mean I don't love you, you blockhead."

"She's never said she loves me," Agustin said.

"Have you asked her?"

No. He hadn't.

He just heard her say that she didn't want a relationship, so that's how he'd interpreted it.

"It's complicated," he said, again, knowing it was just an excuse for his fear.

Fear of falling in love.

Fear of losing.

The problem was, he was in love with her and he was ruining it.

"It's not complicated," Sandrine said. "It really isn't. Make it right, Agustin. Or it won't just be me coming after you, but your mother too."

The threat was clear.

He just hoped he hadn't ruined it all.

Sharon was fuming and hurt, but she swallowed all those feelings of pain and betrayal as she assisted the nursing staff in the hospital as they cared for all the victims of the major pileup. The emergency crews were still digging people out of the rubble.

It was a mess.

Sharon focused on work and not her broken heart.

Has he really broken your heart, though? Aren't you to blame too?

Agustin wasn't completely to blame. She was too.

All he'd done was something kind to ease the burden off her. Yes, she had the means to solve it, but was she so untrusting that she had to push everyone away? Even the community that loved her abuela as much as she did?

As she glanced around the full emergency room, she could see a community rallying together in the face of tragedy.

Just like her aunt had come for her, and that nurse who had been so kind to her as a child, the nurse who had inspired her to help others.

Her aunt and her abuela always said she took too much on. She never let anyone in and tried to solve every problem herself.

It was true.

She could rely on herself and had always done so.

She couldn't accept any help and she was terrified he was leaving. It was easier to push him away, except there was a part of her that didn't want him out of her life.

A part of her that wanted to rely on him and trust him.

Despite the terror of loving and losing, she was in love with him.

"Victim is male, approximately sixteen to eighteen. Pulled from under a pile of rocks. Burn and crush injuries to the face and neck," a paramedic shouted, pushing the gurney into the trauma bay. He was listing out vitals as Sharon went to help. The boy was lucky to be alive. Then she recognized the shoes. They were distinctive cross trainers Sandrine's boyfriend wore.

Oh, no.

"Victim has identification," a doctor said. "He's Diego Santos. Someone contact his next of kin."

Sharon's stomach twisted. "I know him."

The doctor turned to her. "You do?"

"He's my neighbor's boyfriend," Sharon said.

The doctor nodded. "His face is partially crushed. He needs surgery. Stat."

"I can help," Agustin said, not saying anything to her. Not that she blamed him.

They had both said things. Hurtful things.

Agustin examined him. "He needs surgery. Now. I need an operating room prepped."

"I can help," Sharon offered.

"It'll be a long surgery. You shouldn't be standing that long."

"I'm fine," she said quickly. "This is my job. I can handle it."

"Of course," he replied. "You don't need approval. Prep the patient."

He moved out of the trauma room to get

ready for surgery. It hurt and she wanted to talk to him, but right now they needed to save Diego's life.

Sharon could feel the sweat trickling down her spine under her scrubs. The surgery was grueling and she was getting tired. She was annoyed that she had lost control of her body in this moment. It was a surgery she had never witnessed before and Agustin was a master of it.

"Are you okay, Sharon?" Agustin asked, not looking up from his work.

"Fine," she responded. Only she wasn't completely sure.

"You can take a break," he offered.

She wanted to retort back that she didn't need to, but that seemed a little hotheaded and she wondered where that thought had come from. Her feet began to ache and it felt like her shoes were too tight. She felt off.

"You know what, that might be wise," she admitted.

"Abril, can you take over for Sharon?" Agustin asked.

"Of course, Agustin," Nurse Abril said.

Sharon stepped away and exited the operating room. She scrubbed out and realized she'd been standing there for eight hours. No wonder her shoes were feeling tight—her feet were aching and swollen.

Her head spun, just for a moment, and then she got control of it again. She left the operating room floor and made her way to Sandrine's room.

"Can I come in?" Sharon asked, knocking.

"Sure!" Sandrine said. "You look tired."

"We were in surgery." Sharon didn't want to tell Sandrine who it was. That was up to Agustin. Sharon sat on the edge of Sandrine's bed. "How are you?"

"Fine." Sandrine sighed. "I'm sorry if I had a part in upsetting you, Sharon. It's just we all love your abuela. She delivered most of the neighborhood and beyond, and the community loves you too. I love you."

Sharon smiled. "I love you too, Sandrine. No matter what happens."

"So you're not mad at me?" Sandrine asked.

"No. It's all fine. I was being stubborn. I got it in my head not to receive any help."

Sandrine nodded. "About my brother…he just lost a lot…you know?"

Sharon nodded. "I know. It's just hard for me to trust after my father left."

"Like my mother left." Sandrine sighed. "Not that she was much of one when she was around."

Sharon laughed to herself. "So many coincidences. So many parallels."

Sandrine smiled. "Fate. We're meant to be a family."

And Sharon wanted to believe it, but she still had doubts.

"Agustin loved his wife. What if I'm not enough?" Because she hadn't been enough for her father to stay.

Sandrine shook her head. "He's being stubborn. He won't leave. Please, Sharon, you love him. I know it. Don't be mad at him. He means well."

"I know..." The room began to spin, and her head began to throb with the start of a headache. An excruciating one that was like hot, blinding pain. A knife slicing through her head, stealing her vision. She clutched her head, groaning.

"Sharon?" Sandrine asked.

"Call for help," Sharon managed to get out before everything went black.

Agustin came out of Diego's surgery. He would be fine—he would have some scarring and require physical therapy, but he would live. Agustin had learned from Sandrine and others about Diego's heroics. He had been really wrong about Diego. He'd been wrong about a lot of things.

Now he was looking for Sharon. They had some things to talk about and he hoped that she wasn't still so angry at him.

He wasn't angry with her. It was just a mis-understanding.

He knew she'd needed rest, but that was two hours ago. He'd thought she would've returned to the operating room.

She never did come back and now he was worried. When he came out of the scrub room Dr. Perez, Sharon's OB/GYN, was in scrubs and approached him.

Immediately his heart sank.

Oh, God. No.

"Dr. Perez?" he asked, hoping his voice didn't crack.

"They told me you'd be here. It's about Sharon."

"What's wrong?" he asked, cursing himself inwardly for having let her work, but there had been no way to stop her.

"She has preeclampsia. I've been trying to bring down her blood pressure. It's not budging. The baby is in danger and so is Sharon. I'm prepping the operating room for an emergency C-section."

Agustin's stomach knotted.

The baby could die.

Sharon could die, or would if they didn't proceed with the surgery.

He couldn't lose Sharon.

Not after just finding her. Not after truly realizing after all this time he loved her.

"The baby is twenty-eight weeks," he numbly said, trying to process it all.

"And Sharon's been given some injections to help the baby's lungs. Twenty-eight weeks is not ideal, but it's better than twenty-seven or twenty-six even. Every week matters."

"Can I see her?" Agustin asked.

He needed to tell her how he felt before she went into surgery. She needed to know that he loved her in case… He didn't even want to think about the *in case* because he refused to let it happen.

"Quickly," Dr. Perez said. "She's in the pre-operative area."

Agustin ran to the preoperative ward and found Sharon behind the curtains in a bed, crying softly.

"Querida," he whispered, pushing back the curtains, hoping his voice didn't crack. He was trying to remain strong for her.

She turned to him. "Oh, Agustin. I'm sorry for everything I said."

"Hush." He sat down next to her and took her hand. "No apologies. I'm sorry."

"I'm so worried. She's so small," Sharon whispered.

"She's strong, like her mother." He touched her belly.

Please live, his heart was saying.

Pleading to God and the universe that he hadn't ruined everything by not seeing his second chance when it had been staring him right in the face. He wanted to weep and beg for her survival, for the baby, but right now he had to be strong for her.

"About…everything," she said, mumbling as the medication began to work on her.

"We'll talk later. I'll be here waiting for you, *querida*. I will not leave."

Sharon drifted off as the sedatives began to take over.

"I love you," she whispered.

"I love you too." He kissed her hand as the nurses came to take her into surgery.

His eyes stung with unshed tears. His heart was breaking, watching her being wheeled away and knowing there was nothing he could do.

He was powerless.

He'd sworn he'd never let his heart be hurt again, and here it was breaking, but he wouldn't change anything. Sharon was his second chance at happiness. He could make his home with her.

Anywhere she was, was home.

But now the very scary realization that he may lose her and their baby—it was too much.

Please.

It was a simple prayer.

Just let her live.

He paced outside the operating room. She was under general anesthetic so they wouldn't let him in. Even though he was a surgeon and would be used to seeing a patient under general, because she was his partner, they wouldn't allow him to be there.

So he waited.

And he hated every excruciating minute of it.

Finally her doctor came out.

"She made it," Dr. Perez stated. "She lost a lot of blood, but she'll recover."

"And the baby?" Agustin asked.

"Go in and see for yourself. They're readying her for her transport to the neonatal intensive care unit."

Agustin put on a mask and headed into the operating room. Sharon had been taken to the postanesthesia recovery unit, but the pediatric team was working on his tiny daughter.

She was in an isolette, already hooked up

to machines, but one little eye opened as he squatted to peer in through the glass.

A sob welled up in his throat.

"*Hola*, little one," he murmured, touching the glass and wishing that he could touch her delicate little arm. So tiny, so fragile, but his.

"She's strong, Dr. Varela," a pediatric nurse said.

"Like her mama," Agustin responded, not tearing his gaze from the little life he'd made with Sharon. His daughter was everything, and just as beautiful as her mother. She was love, hope and family.

Everything he'd always wanted but never thought he would have.

And the moment that little baby looked at him through the glass of the isolette, she was his world. Sharon and the baby were his world and he was never letting them go.

Sharon woke up. She felt pain, but she was confused as to why. Then she remembered.

Oh, my God. My baby.

She struggled to open her eyes under the influence of anesthetic. She drifted off again and then woke, not remembering why she was agitated.

"Agustin?" she called out.

"I'm here. Don't worry. I'm not going anywhere."

She sighed and her vision came into focus. He was by her bedside.

"What happened?"

"You had preeclampsia. You had an emergency C-section."

She shook her head. "No. I was working with you on Diego."

"He's fine. He'll live," Agustin said.

All the memories came back to her—the headache, her swollen feet and dizziness. Sandrine calling for help.

"Our baby? You said I had an emergency C-section."

"Yes, you did, and our baby is fine. She's alive and strong."

"Really?" Sharon began to cry. "You saw her?"

"Sí." He took her hand and kissed it. "We can go see her when you're ready."

"I want to go."

He nodded. "I'll get a wheelchair."

Sharon was in pain, but none of that mattered. She wanted to see her baby. She took her time and slowly sat up.

Agustin helped her out of bed. She used a pillow to brace her incision. He helped with her IV bag. She slowly sat down. Once she was settled, he tucked a blanket around her and wheeled her through the halls to the other end of the hospital where the neonatal intensive care unit was.

Her heart was swelling with joy and fear. All these emotions going through her. She was trying to hold them back. To be strong.

Agustin took her to the isolette in the corner of the unit. Under all the wires and lines, there was a tiny baby.

Her baby.

So small, with just a whisper of dark hair.

"See our daughter, *querida*. She's strong," Agustin said proudly.

"I see," Sharon said, her voice trembling as she tentatively reached out and touched the glass, wishing that she could hold her.

"Would you like to hold her, Sharon?" the nurse asked. "Skin to skin, or kangaroo care, is great for preemies. She's doing well."

"Yes," Sharon whispered.

Her heart ached to hold her, because holding her meant that she would be okay. At least in her mind. Holding her daughter would let her little girl know that she hadn't left her. She wasn't alone and she would never feel that longing, that pain for want of a parent who didn't want them.

The nurse gently took her tiny baby out.

Sharon moved her hospital gown aside and her little girl, who curled up in the palm of the nurse's hand, was placed on her skin. A tangle of cords, but warm as Sharon cradled her close to her heart.

"Her stats are already improving," Agustin remarked.

The nurse smiled. "Kangaroo is the best. I'll leave you two. Let me know when you want to take Sharon back up to her room and I'll put the baby back. Sharon needs to rest too. She just had major surgery," the nurse reminded them, because Sharon knew that the nurse knew that doctors and nurses made the worst patients.

Agustin knelt down beside them. He was smiling, his eyes twinkling. A tear slid down his cheek and he brushed it away quickly.

"Agustin, are you crying?" Sharon asked.

"Sí."

"Why?"

"Because this is the most beautiful thing. It brings me joy that I didn't think was possible again. I almost ruined it. I will do better. I love you, Sharon. I can't lose you."

"What about your work and your grief?" she asked, stunned.

"The only plans I have involve you, our baby, your abuela and Sandrine. And I guess my mother and Javier, but those plans are here in Ushuaia. Luisa has been gone a long time. I will always love her and miss her, my heart will always hold her, but there's room for you. For more love. She would want me to be happy. I believe she sent me to you."

Sharon grinned. She couldn't hold back the tears. "I love you and I tried to push you away. I thought it would be easier if I pushed you away instead of waiting for you to leave."

"I'd never leave you, *querida*. Both of you are my life." He leaned over and kissed her. "Say you'll marry me?"

"Yes." Her heart overflowed with joy. "I love you, Agustin, and I'm sorry too. I just want you. I'm scared about the future, but I am more terrified about a future without you."

"Agreed. I can't live without you or her." Agustin kissed her again and they both gazed down at the little life squirming and moving against her chest. "What shall we name her?"

"How about Ava Theresa after your mother and my abuela? Both strong women."

His eyes twinkled. "Perfection."

"*Sí.* Perfection." She gazed down at her little miracle and then to the man that she loved. It was all a little too much and she really couldn't hold back the joy she was feeling, sitting here holding her little girl.

She couldn't quite believe that she was here. That this little surprise had happened to her. This was never in the plans. She never thought that love would find her or come looking for her like it had, but she knew one thing—with Agustin and her little daughter in her arms, she was home.

For the first time in her life she felt like this was really home. She was no longer that little girl, scared, living on cereal in an apartment waiting for her father to come home, moving between her aunt's and her abuela's. Her whole life she had been lost and floating, but now this was home.

Finally, she was home.

It had taken so long to get here and there'd been many surprises along the way, like a pregnancy, but they were good surprises. They were what she'd needed to find her path and wake up from that nightmare of her past that had held her heart captive for too long.

She was finally home.

She had finally found her family.

She had found her forever family at the end of the world.

EPILOGUE

Six months later

SHARON GLANCED OUT the window at the shared garden between her abuela's house and Agustin's house, which had been his childhood home. There was construction to join the two homes together and expand so that they wouldn't have to walk outside to visit her abuela, who was doing so much better and didn't require as much care.

Abuela's home would be a small, contained apartment, but without a kitchen. Abuela would be coming across to the main house and having dinner with them, which suited her abuela fine.

Her abuela reveled in her great-granddaughter and namesake.

Sandrine loved having the homes connected.

She would be off to Buenos Aires in a year

to go to school and living with Ava and Javier at Agustin's insistence.

Sandrine was going through school to be a surgeon, like her big brother. This time, it was her choice.

For now, Sandrine soaked up every moment of being a doting auntie. Sharon smiled at Sandrine curled up next to little Ava Theresa, who was trying to learn to crawl. She was up on all fours and rocking back and forth as Sandrine coaxed her from the other side of the blanket.

Her abuela was sitting outside under the pergola Agustin had installed so they would have some shade from the sun. She was clapping and cheering little Ava Theresa on too.

And Agustin's mother, who was down for a visit, was setting out a light lunch. They were going to have a picnic when Javier showed up.

A family picnic.

Sharon never thought she would ever really get to experience that with her own little family unit, but that was what she had here in Ushuaia and it made her heart burst with happiness watching them all.

It was the perfect late summer day.

Agustin came up behind her and slipped his arms around her. "What're you looking at?"

"Just enjoying the view," she remarked, wrapping her arms around his.

He leaned his head on her shoulder. "Is she trying to crawl?"

"I think so."

Agustin moved away, panicked that he was going to miss a milestone. "I don't have my camera."

Sharon laughed. "Sandrine has it. Don't worry, she'll catch it all. Between you and your sister, Ava's life is going to be completely documented from dawn to dusk for the next twenty years."

Agustin chuckled and then spun her around to face him, touching her face. "How did I get so lucky?"

"I believe it was the elevator at the conference hotel where we first met," she said teasingly. "Of course, it could've been that workshop on infections."

"I do remember that, but I mostly recall the kiss on the beach and afterward." He grinned.

"Oh, I remember that too. Fondly."

He chuckled. "Have I told you lately that I love you like crazy?"

"Not lately."

He kissed her, but their kiss was interrupted by the sound of the doorbell. Agustin groaned. "It's probably him."

"Be nice. You saved his life. Besides, I thought you liked him now. He's a hero."

"I know, I know, but I can't let him know that."

"You need to be nicer. Show him that you like him."

"Am I supposed to like the boyfriend?" Agustin groused.

Sharon crossed her arms. "Yes. Especially when he adores you for what you did. He's here today because of you."

Agustin groaned, but smiled and opened the door. "Mr. Santos, you're right on time."

Diego smiled brightly. It was only a half smile as he had some nerve damage and he walked with a slight limp, but he no longer needed his cane thanks to Sharon helping him as much as she could when he was over visiting Sandrine.

"My mother sent asados," Diego said, holding up the plate.

"Those look delicious!" Sharon exclaimed, taking the plate. "Have you been practicing your walking in the pool downtown?"

"Yes, Sharon," Diego replied, smiling.

Sharon nodded. "Good. Sandrine is outside with Ava…or both Avas."

Diego grinned and made his way through the house and through the new sliding glass doors out into the back garden.

Agustin's mom got Diego a chair and fussed

over him. Sharon watched as Sandrine stood up, bent down and gave him a kiss. She could see the love there. They were young, but it was undeniable.

Sandrine had been crushed when she learned Diego had almost died, but he'd pulled through and Sharon couldn't help but wonder if in a few years' time they would be having a little wedding out there.

"What're you thinking about now?" Agustin asked.

"Weddings," she responded dreamily.

"You don't mean my little sister and Diego?" Agustin groused.

Sharon laughed. "In a few years. Once she's a surgeon. Then she can have two flower girls, or a flower girl and a ring bearer."

Agustin's eyes widened. "What're you telling me?"

Sharon had taken the test that morning. They'd had the all-clear from Dr. Perez that they could try for another baby. Initially Sharon had missed the signs again, but thankfully she'd figured things out quicker this time around—only six weeks this time. She held up the test for him.

"I'm six weeks. At least I'm not twenty. By next June or July we should have a full-term addition to the family."

Agustin kissed her. "I think I'm in shock. Another winter baby!" He smiled. "I'm extremely happy."

"Are you?" she asked.

He scooped her up in his arms and she squealed as he kissed her passionately, making her blood heat in anticipation.

"Let me show you exactly how happy I am," he said huskily.

"Yes, show me, but be quick about it...we have guests."

"Quick? I don't do quick," he murmured against her neck.

She melted a bit. "Okay, fine, but we don't have all day."

His eyes gleamed. "Who says we don't?"

Her knees went weak. "I can't resist you, Agustin."

"And I can't resist you either, *querida*." Agustin winked and carried her up the stairs to their very private, newly finished master suite and the large king bed. He showed her exactly how he was feeling about the new baby. The new surprise they weren't expecting, but one that was welcome all the same.

Just another person to add to their family.

A family full of love.

* * * * *

*If you enjoyed this story, check out
these other great reads from
Amy Ruttan*

Winning the Neonatal Doc's Heart
Paramedic's One-Night Baby Bombshell
The Doctor She Should Resist
A Ring for His Pregnant Midwife

All available now!